MOON

OVER

SPUTNIK

by

R. P. Poncy

Books by R.P. Poncy

The Wishing Stick

Sans Souls

Indivisible

Benjamin Brown

This book is dedicated to
Sergei Korolev

He brought the world into our living
rooms

ISBN-13# 978-0615703978 ISBN-10# 0615703976
Library of Congress Catalog # applied for

Grey Knight Press
mail@greyknightpress.com

1

So there I was, standing on the back shelf with my hands over my balls. I looked to see if Jerry was watching, but he wasn't, so I took my hands away. I was a pin boy over at my old man's place, an eight-lane job in central Jersey. So was my older brother, Ted. Except lately the old man had promoted Ted to be the foul line guy. What a cushy job that is. You just sit there in a stupid chair and sight along the foul line, and if you see a guy slip across the line then, bingo! you yell "FOUL!" Except Ted never did. He was much too chicken. I once asked the old man if I could do it instead, but he said it was "too much responsibility" or some shit-ass excuse like that. I didn't buy it. The fact of the matter is, the old man favored Ted over me, and not just because he's older. He's always saying how proud he is of that guy, and to me how I need to get my act together. How can I do that, if he doesn't give *me* responsibility?

"He never even calls a foul!" I yelled.

"Don't yell at me!" the old man had said. "Ted does a good job."

I shot back, "Pops, he doesn't go a good job, he Does a *perfect* job. He's O *fer*."

"Quit being such a wise guy," the old man had hollered back. And that was the end of that.

Not that pin setting is a no responsibility job, mind you. In fact, it was a hell of a lot more responsibility than that stupid foul line job, and it was a constant thing, not like a once-in-a-while thing like the foul line job. But like I said, Ted made it a never-in-a-while thing.

The men's Saturday night spring bowling league was really heating up. All eight lanes stayed busy from seven till closing with two leagues, one right after the other. During these busy nights, my old lady helped out. The old man couldn't afford to hire an extra person to serve drinks and snacks and stuff, so he had my mom do it. I think she always hated the job; in fact I know she did. Spending a Saturday night in a smoke filled bowling alley full of half drunk assholes just wasn't her cup of tea. At least she got to spend it with her family, I guess. Come to think of it, Ted tended to be a real asshole too, so there was one more she could spend time with. I laughed at that thought.

I'd never asked for the details, but I'd heard enough to know my dad had been a war hero. Just after Ted came along, the good old USA had entered the war after Pearl Harbor, and the old man was in the army and shipped out. I'd once overheard my old lady tell Ted about how the old man had wanted to be a doctor; he'd told her so when they were just kids growing up together, but that when they got married real young, well, that had put a bump I guess you could say in those plans, and the war had snuffed them out altogether. The old man was twenty-two by the time he came home, and there were too many responsibilities by then to worry about going to school and whatever else you had to do to become a doc. I think it's all bullshit, if you ask me. I mean, what kind of a guy wouldn't be a doc, and then open up some pinhole sized bowling alley? I don't mean to be tough on the old man, but come on. Who are we trying to fool here? Not me. Ted probably buys it, but I sure don't.

Anyway, I was working two lanes, numbers four and five. I was an old pro, really good, in fact. I could set 'em up as good as any fellow. It seemed that on these busy nights, we were always short at least one good pin boy, and, in fact, we were short two. So the old man put two punks, one on either side of me, in case they needed help, which was laughable since I had my hands full what with two lanes. They each only worked one. My good buddy Lance worked lanes one and two, and Jerry was working seven and eight. They were old pros like me. I kind of took pride in them, sure enough. I taught them everything they knew, bowling wise that is. I was wishing Ted was here beside me, instead of these two punks, and then things would be a piece of cake. It seemed a waste having him set there in that chair, doing nothing, for Christ's sake. One a'them punks on either side of me could have been doing what he was doing, which was nothing.

Things moved fast in the pit. Near every moment, pins are flying on at least one lane. BANG! It never stopped, and it was loud as hell. But you got used to it.

A ball came rolling down lane four and struck the pins. Five went down. I hopped down from the shelf, shoved the fallen pins out of the way, and picked the ball up and sent it on its way back. I heard a crash of pins on lane five, hopped over there, and since this one had been a strike, I had to set all ten of them up and be right quick about it.

For this the old man paid us five cents a string, or ten frames, per bowler. Ted was making more than I did, I think, the shit. And for doing nothing, besides. Every time he reached down and took a swig of his bottle of soda pop, I felt like bopping him over the head with it. Like he got thirsty, or something, just sitting there like he did. One night in bed before I'd fallen asleep, I'd thought about what I could do with that extra money he made. I'd imagined Bazooka gums each with the Bazooka Joe comic in it, or the wax bottles with that drink inside, whatever the hell it was, or the candy dots, and maybe even save a penny or two while I was at it. Or even save enough so my old lady wouldn't have to be here anymore with all us losers.

"Danny, I can't do this near fast enough," I heard this whiny, pipsqueak voice from behind me.

"Christ, kid," I said, setting up some pins. "I got my hands full with two lanes, can't you see?"

"Yeah, but you been doin this-" he started to say but his voice got drowned out by the pins flying around. I figured he'd said 'forever' or something stupid like that. He probably didn't say 'kid' even though I was still a kid, of course, but then again, this pipsqueak punk looked to me to be about eight, so to him I must have looked like an adult or something.

A minute later, things went quiet as the first games of the nine o'clock league had ended. The kid was perched on the back shelf, rubbing his shin.

"Christ, kid," I said. "What the hell you doin' here, anyway?" Don't your folks know you'll be here till past eleven? What kind of parents you got anyway, to leave the puny likes of you out by yourself, doin' this shit?"

"'Course they know," he said. "That's my old man out there," he said, pointing.

I looked out at the bowlers. Most were at the tables behind the lanes, some others and some spectator sorts were at the bar with my old man, who was behind it. I couldn't hardly make out the far end of the bar not for distance but because the goddamn smoke was so thick.

"Which one? Which one's your old man?" I squinted.

"My shin hurts bad, Danny," the punk said.

"You've got to pick it up kid, pick you're legs up quick, or you'll get nicked.

"I do, but I get hit anyway. You know, sometimes they throw the second ball before you get clear out of the way"

"Yeah, I know," I said. "It's that asshole, Kowalski. He-"

"That's my dad, Danny," he was saying, but I wasn't listening, I guess.

"-makes a game of it. Which one did you say?"

"He's my dad," the punk said, pointing again.

"Which one, kid?"

"I just *told* you, Danny. Kowalski."

"What?" I asked.

"Danny," the kid said. "I'm *trying* to tell you I'm a Kowalski. My dad's Kowalski.

I peered out again into the haze, and saw Kowalski moving his stuff over to lane four. "You mean your old man's Kowalski?"

"That's what I've been trying to say!"

"Your old man hit you, didn't he?"

"Why no, one a' these pins did."

"Oh Christ kid," I said. "Don't get technical on me. You know what the hell I mean. He threw his damn ball while you were still in the pit, didn't he?"

"You shouldn't be talkin' about my dad that way, Danny, you know?" the kid said.

"Christ!" I said. "Now he's coming over to *my* lane!"

"Ha Ha! Danny boy!" I heard Jerry yell out from the end of the shelf over at lane eight. "You got Kowalski now!"

I honestly hadn't noticed where Kowalski had been bowling, and that his own kid had gotten stuck setting pins for him. I watched as he took a swig of beer and moved his big ass over to my lane, and he half turned to look back at my mom. Her skirt swished by him, and she was holding a tray full of drinks.

"Heh, heh, Barb," I heard him say, and he reached out and pinched her. She jumped away and damn near pitched everything over, and I heard her squeal. He laughed again. I'd never noticed him or anyone else ever do that to her before, and wondered whether it was the first time. I hoped so. I swear I could have killed him just then. I felt like running over to him and smashing a ball over his stinking head. I glanced over at my old man, but I don't think he had noticed any of it. My mom ignored it. I doubt if she'd say anything to him about it.

God, she *was* cute! Damn cute, what with that skirt she had on down to the top of her ankles and the red sneakers and white bobbies. I didn't have to say it; everybody knew it. But she was my old lady, goddamn it, and Kowalski or any other asshole had no right to touch her, except my old man, of course.

I felt the kid looking at me. "Sorry, Danny. That's just my dad. He does those sort of things. He don't mean nuthin' by it, I swear he don't." The kid looked scared. I felt badly for him, just then.

"Ain't your fault, kid," I said. "What's your name, anyway?"

"Francis, but everybody calls me Pete," kid Kowalski said.

"How the hell you end up with a name like that?"

"Which?"

"Which," I mocked. I was being a smartass, I know. "*Francis.*"

"Oh. My mom, she likes it, I guess. But my middle name is what everybody calls me, on account of that's what I tell everybody my name is. Usually I don't even mention my first name, but I figured you might want to know, maybe," he said, and shrugged. He was a funny kid.

"What about your old lady? What's she got to say about all this?"

"Don't know. She done left us just last week. That's why you never saw me before, guess that means she wouldn't like it at all, I guess."

I turned away from him and gazed back at his old man. I think I knew why she left, I wanted to say, but of course, I didn't. I can be a real shit just like the next guy, but not that bad of one. I wondered why she'd left her kid behind too.

I glanced at my Timex and it said near ten. John Cameron Swayze or whatever the hell his fancy name is, says they keep on ticking after taking a licking, but that's just rhyming bull crap, if you ask me. There ain't no such watch like that. I remembered an ad I saw in a magazine somewhere featuring The Mick where he had one of these

Timex stretched around the barrel of his bat. You were supposed to think it kept ticking after swinging the lumber, I guess, although I don't think it could take a direct hit from a ball. There was no goddamn way. I sometimes wondered what would happen if a pin came up into mine and hit it head on, but it hadn't happened yet. A few came pretty close, though.

I'd lost track of the frames, but then the yell came for the tenth. That was how you knew a bowler might throw a bunch of balls before sitting down.

I'd been nicked twice already, both times by that asshole Kowalski, once while on the shelf, and once while I was still in the pit. He was such a bastard. The pin had come up and hit me square in the left side, and I thought I'd busted a rib. It was hard to believe he'd purposely hit the pin boys, but what did you expect when he hit his own kid? And it didn't bother him that my folks were behind him, I guess.

"Hey kid," I said over to kid Kowalski, who was standing next to me on the shelf. We only took the luxury of sitting between games, otherwise a pin could come up and hit us in the head. Although once, Jerry took one in the nuts and he went down. That's why I sometimes hold my hands over them, and look over at him to see if he's looking at me just to be funny like, as I'd said before. He'd been working the lanes next to me that night when I heard him sucking wind, like some kind of old geezer who smoked all day long. I'd looked up and he was cupping his balls, and he clear fainted, and fell like heavy timber, straight like. I'll never forget that moment when he toppled right onto the standing five pin, and took *that* right in the nuts, but I don't think he felt it since he was already out cold. I swear he was suspended on top of it perfectly, like some sort of seesaw, and then he pitched forward and took the standing three pin in the forehead.

I'd gone over to him and asked the stupidest question in the history of the world, which was, "You all right?" They might as well have asked that to one of those guys on the cross when they crucified the poor bastard.

The ambulance had come and hauled him away. His old lady had been hysterical, naturally. How she'd let him work the lanes after that I can't guess, but it must've been one hell of a persuasion job on his part, unless he lied about ever coming back here. He usually kept a smile on his face doing near everything, even standing on the shelf. Once in a while when we eyed each other he'd give me a wink. He was a funny kid, and you couldn't help but like him. And he was tough as pin lumber, apparently.

Anyway, I said, "Hey kid," and kid Kowalski looked over at me.

"Yeah?" he asked.

"How old are you, anyways?"

"Ten."

"You're awfully small, 'specially since your old man is such a huge ass." I was mad as hell about his old man, so I didn't mind calling him that in front of his kid. Pins went down and we hopped off the shelf.

"My mom, she's small," he said. "But my mom says I'll start growin' real soon."

The kid was clearing pins when I thought I heard a good sniff. Christ, he was beginning to cry.

"Hey, kid!" some bastard yelled. "Get the hell outta' the way, 'fore I throw this goddamn ball and break you're fuckin' head!"

"Oh Danny," he was saying, " My mom ain't gonna' see me grow!"

"Kid, pick yourself up! Get the hell back on the shelf!" I yelled.

But he couldn't or wouldn't; he was too far gone. He was collapsed in a heap of sorrow, bawling like a baby. I picked him up. He seemed light as a feather.

"C'mon, kid." I helped him back to the shelf. I heard a ball make contact with a lane, never thinking it was the kid's lane. I turned to look, and the goddamn ball was coming right towards me. I jumped up next to the kid just in the nick of time before the ball slammed into the back wall. It was some jerk named Bender. He was almost as bad as Kowalski.

The kid recovered after that. He seemed to come to somehow, even better than before. He worked his ass off and was no problem. His brain had snapped to it, for some reason. Maybe he was just real pissed off, like I was.

The last game came around. The smoke was so thick in the joint you could barely see where the tables were. Once in a while, I'd see my mom appear out from the haze like a ghost and then disappear again.

The bowlers kept getting louder and louder. They were hooting it up real good as things were getting near the end.

The two best bowlers in the league by far were that asshole Kowalski and a loser by the name of Snodgrass. Actually I didn't know the old man, but his kid was a real loser asshole, so I figured his old man had to be too. They were all loser assholes when you came down to it. Who else would be bowling on a Saturday night? I mean, why weren't these guys with their families, or something?

Both these guys had averages over two hundred every goddamn yeahr. They hated each other, and were out there now bowling against one another. In fact, both these teams hated each other. Kowalski and the rest of his bunch were union electrical guys, members of the brotherhood. You could tell them a mile away because they always had those stupid IBEW shirts on wherever they went, and those stupid IBEW stickers all over the place. And they picked a real stupid name for their team: The Lightning Bolts. How dumb is that? The other guys were non-union, and just had regular jobs. They called themselves the Knockers. What the hell a knocker was beat the hell out of me.

Anyway, my Timex said something past eleven, but what exactly I couldn't tell. I had so much sweat poring into my eyes I couldn't see straight. What made it worse was that I'd knocked my bottle of soda pop over in the second frame, so it'd been a while since my last swig

"Can I help, Danny?" the kid was asking me, both of us on the back shelf again. It was then that I realized he had nothing to do; in fact, all the other lanes had gone quiet. They'd all finished their games except my guys.

We came to the tenth, and I knew the match was close. You can always tell. The guys were screaming with every shot, back and forth like.

"Atta boy!" some asshole would yell. "One more!" and that kind of crap.

I figured it would come down to the last two, the captains, Kowalski and that Snodgrass guy.

Snodgrass started his tenth, while Kowalski's teammates finished up. I hopped up on the shelf. Snodgrass was a lefty, so he let his ball fly with a loud pop down my right side, and as usual, it came real close to edging into the gutter, but of course it didn't go in. It hooked nicely towards the pocket and the pins scattered like matchsticks.

"You'd better get two more of those, Snodgrass," Kowalski was yelling, heh, heh, and looking over at his teammates with a stupid grin on his face. I wanted to push it in. He was polishing his ball real good, waiting to start his tenth until Snodgrass was done.

"Shut the hell up," someone said from the Knockers.

"Shut up, you!" another guy said from the back somewhere.

"Hey cut it out, all of you, just bowl!" I could hear the old man yell from way back.

My mom had moved forward to better watch the action. Somehow, I swear, she'd never looked so beautiful. Somehow she always managed to look so damn pretty, no matter what the situation, and you had to figure this joint was the worst situation you could think of for some broad to look pretty in. She stood tall, feet together straight ahead with them red shoes and bobby socks. Her skirt and hair looked perfect still, like she'd just come out from her bathroom back home. She must have really loved my old man to always look like that.

And for the first time, I couldn't quite figure that out. I knew right then and there how much she didn't belong. I hate to say it, but she deserved better than the likes of the old man and the rest of us, her brood I mean. She deserved to be in some quiet place right now, maybe out to dinner with some swank guy in some swank joint with soft music. It was like she was stuck in the wrong movie. The wrong cast of characters. I think she knew what I was thinking just then, I swear, because she was staring straight at me.

"Hey kid, set'em up!" Snodgrass was yelling. What an asshole, he could have addressed me by my name; everybody knew me, especially with my parents right there. I looked down from the shelf. All the pins had scattered.

I looked down at his ball, and went to pick it up from the back wall. I couldn't believe what I was seeing. Stuck down into the first finger hole was a dollar bill. Snodgrass was paying me to set the pins a wee bit closer to help with the last strike. It'd been done before, to me I mean. Sure I'd tighten up the formation, but careful like. I was glad to do it against the likes of that asshole Kowalski.

I obliged him all right, and turned away to tuck the bill into my pocket so nobody could see. I sent his ball back. He readied himself. He tossed the ball, real nice as usual. The ball caught the pocket, but wouldn't you know, he was a victim of the seven-pin tap, despite my doings.

"We're ok," a guy said on his team. "We're still in it."

Kowalski finished polishing his stupid ball. I thought he'd have wiped the whole damn thing down to nothing by now. He tossed his towel and took some rosin. I didn't know what he needed for his team to win.

He set himself, and tossed the ball with a pop. Kowalski, who was a righty, didn't have quite the hook

Snodgrass did, so he started it out like always on the second board in. It came in real nice, and all the pins flew.

"One more baby!" a guy behind him yelled.

I set the pins and sent his ball back and hopped up on the shelf. I looked over at Jerry, who now was sitting nearby next to kid Kowalski. He had a big shit-eating grin on his face. "I saw you cup that dollar, Danny boy."

"Shhh!" I shot back. "They'll hear you, asshole!"

He kept grinning, of course, and gave me a wink.

Kowalski took up his ball, wiped it, and threw his towel aside. He flipped the rosin up and down, and powder flew. I had to admit, the guy was a hell of a bowler. You had to admire a guy like that, even if he was a complete jerk. I mean, he stuck to his routine. He was a goddamn pro, if you ask me. He put his fingers in the holes and looked down at his feet. He didn't need a strike, but he obviously hadn't won yet. But I don't think he needed much.

Pop, thud, and the ball came rolling and spinning towards me. For some reason, his right foot came into real sharp focus, almost like I had a telescope or something. It slid forward, like in slow motion, and kept sliding and came to a stop clearly ahead of the foul line. I picked up the flight of the ball, and it was coming in low. You can tell real quick after you'd seen a billion balls come roaring towards you. It caught the three pin to the outside, which was to his advantage, given all the action it would cause. The pins slid all over the place cutting down the standing ones sloppy like. The electricians went nuts. They were really whooping it up.

My eyes slid over to Ted, who just sat there still as stone. Kowalski then lifted his right leg and began to swivel round, and when he came to face Ted he hesitated just a bit, and a stupid grin spread across his face.

It was too goddamn much to take, and I lost it. I hopped off the shelf and ran right down the middle of the lane like some Olympic sprinter, except I was sliding around a bit.

"Foul! You fouled!" I hollered.

Kowalski turned around to face me.

I got three quarters down the lane and stopped. I pointed at the big lout. "You fouled, and you know it!" I said.

No one was saying anything. My old man's bowling alley had quieted like a morgue. Then I noticed my mom, and the tray she was carrying started to pitch forward, and things started to slide off it, and the next thing you know the tray and everything crashed to the floor. It was the loudest sound I'd ever heard.

"You see? You see what I'm talking about, Henry!" Kowalski was saying to my old man, pointing at me. He turned his head to look back at the bar. "You see? These punk kids you got working here don't know their place. I think us boys is gonna' bowl next league over at Rizzuto and Berra's.

Rizzuto and Berra? What the hell was he talking about? *Phil* Rizzuto and *Yogi* Berra?

I don't remember much else that night, except the warm embrace of my mom, and me burying my sorry ass snout into her soft blouse, and the hot tears running down my stupid face.

"Now, now," she was saying, patting my head. It was all very embarrassing.

I think I remember then saying, "Ted, he never calls a foul," or something snivelly like that. I guess I'm not such a tough guy after all.

And I wasn't sure if I was still awake or dreaming my last thoughts after I'd hit the sack, about what the hell Phil Rizzuto and Yogi Berra had to do with any of it.

2

"That was a shitty thing you did last night," Ted said, real snotty like. We shared the same bedroom, and I hadn't even finished waking up yet. He must've waited for me to stir to pounce on me.

That was typical of Ted to feel that way, just like a lot of people I know would. It burns my ass when they don't recognize it when you're doing them a favor, sticking up for them even.

"I was just doing you a favor, sticking up for you. You think I *wanted* to have to do that?" I said.

"Sticking up for me? What the hell are you talking about!" he yelled. He was propped up on his side facing me, I could tell, even though I just stared at the ceiling. I wouldn't look at him.

"Shhhh. Stop yelling!" I yelled, but whisper like. "You'll wake mom and dad."

"Wake them? They've been up for hours. They're really going to let you have it this time, buddy."

I don't know why he had the obnoxious habit of calling me buddy whenever he figured I was in trouble. As far as I was concerned, we weren't buddies.

"If you'd called that foul, none of this would've happened," I said, matter-of-factly. "What time is it, anyway?"

"What foul, you idiot! He never crossed the line! How could you pretend to tell from you're vantage point."

Vantage point. He was always using fancy expressions like that. He was a real snot. "I saw it clearly," I said. "And you didn't call one foul last night, just like you never do. There must've been a million of them."

"You're such an idiot to think I wouldn't call a foul if there was one," he said.

"Look," I said. "You've been on the foul line for what, six Saturdays now, and you ain't called one stinking foul yet. You mean to tell me *no* one has fouled in that stupid league for six weeks? They sure did before then."

"I haven't called any because there haven't been any, you fool," Ted said.

"They happened all right. You're just too chicken to call one against those bums. Kowalski stared you down after he did it, daring you to call it. I caught that, and you froze up, plain and simple."

"You're demented. Dad'll handle you," Ted said, and went off to the bathroom. He always gave up like that, totally defeated by my logic. And he was supposed to be the smart one.

I found out the old man had gone off to the hardware store already, so he couldn't holler at me. Now there's a place for you. I couldn't wait to grow up and spend all my time at the hardware store like all men did. I couldn't figure it out, what with the garage full of hardware crap we already had. I think the old man had at least one of everything the store did, but it was just that he never could find what he was looking for. That was something else I was always getting hollered at about. I never used any of that hardware crap in my life. I hate tools and springs and whatnot, so why would I move them around? Ted used that crap with his tinkering all the time.

I think I'll just buy a hardware store someday, that way I won't have to go to it and have a garage full of the same stuff.

Anyway, my mom didn't say anything about my hi-jinx from the night before, but I could tell she was sore about it. I was eating my breakfast and she said, "You can go over to Mrs. Sweet's when you're finished. She asked if you could help her move some things."

I didn't buy it. This was some sort of punishment. "She asked?"

"Yes, Yesterday morning. Sorry, I forgot to mention it. It will do you good. And please behave, she's a dear old friend of mine."

That's something that pisses me off about people. They ask you to do a favor, and they know if you don't come through you come out looking like a real shit. And I especially hate it when some adult asks your old lady or old man if their kid can do it, namely yours truly.

When I got to her place, the first thing I did was ask her if she had asked my old lady if I could help her move stuff.

"Why, yes, I did Danny," she answered.

"Well, ok, no problem."

"Why, do you have something else to do?" she asked.

"No, I was just wondering, is all." I felt kind of bad doubting my mom's story.

I'd been to the old bag's place once before, maybe four years ago, with the old lady. She was so ancient she used to actually teach my parents in grade school, I think it was. The place had that same type of smell all old people's places had, like a combination of some sort of mold and cabbage. She was very foreign looking. And she dressed like she was stuck in the nineteenth century or something.

We went into the living room where there was a bunch of clunky furniture. What was it about old people and their goddamn furniture anyway? You were never allowed to actually sit on it. I mean you could sit on it but not directly. It was always covered with white sheets or some crap, like if you sat on the stuff the furniture was made of it would disintegrate. Come to think of it, maybe it would, it all looked so damned old.

Plus, they always had boarders. Guys who clopped around upstairs. My grandmother's over in Pennsy was the same way, and you never saw one of them, like they were vampires. It was all very strange, this getting old business, if you ask me. I think when I get old I'll just stay down at the old hardware store.

Anyway, Mrs. Sweet lived a couple blocks from us in a big row house. The shades were mostly always drawn, like they are in all old people's places. They don't like much light, I figured. Maybe it was to protect their damn vampire boarders.

She said I should sit down, so I did. I half disappeared into the cushion. Behind me were two dark brown curtains closed in the middle like in a hospital room.

"So," she said, and sat in a chair next to me. It was then that I noticed her shoes. They looked like they'd been chiseled out of black rock and weighed a ton, like Frankenstein wears in those movies. She had on dark stockings rolled down to her ankles. It was hard to believe she must have been young once. I didn't want to try and imagine it. "I asked your mother if I could borrow you today, and help me with some things in the attic. Bring them down, actually. Do you think you're up to it? They're in boxes."

Clop, clop, clop, Frankenstein the border was upstairs. Where the hell was the guy going, back and forth like that? I knew it wasn't her husband because he was dead. And I was thinking that maybe he was behind that curtain, stuffed and moldy.

"Can I ask you something, Mrs. Sweet?"

"Of course, Daniel, ask away. I was a schoolteacher once, remember?" she said and smiled.

"How come you don't get one of your boarders up there to do it for you? I'm sure they're a lot bigger than me."

She folded her hands. I hate when you ask an adult a question and before they answer they do that. It means the answer's going to be a whopper. She probably sent a shit load of kids to the principal's office after doing that.

"Well, that's a very good question which deserves a good answer. You see, I wanted us to spend time together, and I thought you might enjoy getting them yourself. They're not heavy, I promise."

"Oh," I said. "I see."

"You look uncomfortable," she said. "I won't bite," she laughed.

I laughed too, only phony like. "Well, let's get to it," I said. I wanted to get the hell out of there. "Just tell me the way."

"You go out into the hallway and turn left, go through the kitchen and you'll see the stairway in the back. At the far end of the hallway upstairs you'll see a door. Through there you'll see another flight of stairs and at the top is another door, which leads to the attic. There are four boxes I want you to bring down. They're just inside the door; you'll see them. You'll want to bring them down one at a time, now, and slowly. You wouldn't want to fall and break your neck now, would you?"

I couldn't believe it. I was going to have to go up and down two flights of stairs four times, and for what I couldn't imagine. This was all because of my antics of last night, and I cursed myself. Goddamn it.

I left her and went into the kitchen. Bolted to a table was a meat grinder like my Grandmother has. I gotta' admit, the sausage that came out the side of that thing of my Grandmother's was damn good after she got done cookin' it up. I took the stairs, and when I got to the top, I heard a funny noise coming from the first room on the right. The door was open. I froze. I had to go past that room, but I didn't want to. Not with Frankenstein in it. I started to walk, though, and when I got outside the room I made sure I just kept looking straight ahead.

"Hey ki-. Hey ki-." I heard this voice say, but I kept on going, which was really stupid because if this guy in the room now behind me was some kind of kid killer, then he had me trapped. I came to the end of the hall and opened up the door. It was dark as hell. I could barely make out the first step. I figured there had to be a light and felt along the wall. Sure enough, I found the switch and a dim bare bulb at the top of the stair came on.

The stairs were lined on either side with all kinds of crap, and I had to walk between it all. I opened the door at the top of the stairs and looked behind me, expecting the door at the bottom to slam shut, with just me and the kid killer up there. I didn't like this one bit. I tried to forget about it, and spied the four boxes. The attic had plenty of light from a window. There was more light up here than in the rest of the house.

The roof was low and slanted. Under the window was a small chest of drawers. I figured what the hell, I'd go see what was in it.

I slid open the top drawer and some framed pictures were stacked inside. I pulled out the top one. In the picture was a young couple in their wedding stuff, and some guy and some broad were standing next to them on either side. The bride looked familiar somehow. I knew it had to be the old lady downstairs, Mrs. Sweet. I looked at her closer, and you know, she wasn't half bad looking. She was damned pretty, if you ask me. I took the next one out. It was of her again, and next to her was the same broad as in the other picture. Both of them were in those old fashioned bathing suits like they wore in the last century. I flipped it over and some writing on the back of it said, 'Me and Hilda in Atlantic City 1920.' I couldn't believe I was looking at the same person who was now downstairs, sitting in that clunky chair with all those clunky clothes on. The third picture was of some guy, young and strange looking. He was dressed in a white gown, like something you'd see somebody wear in a hospital. I flipped this one over, and written on the back was, 'Peter 1921.'

I put the pictures back and figured I'd better double time it downstairs or the old bag would think I'd broken my neck, except now the old bag had been replaced in my mind by some hot looking young chick. It was all very confusing.

I picked up the first box and beat it down the stairs and the hallway. A funny noise was coming from that room again.

"Uhhh, uh, uh!" The guy in there was grunting something awful. I knew he could hear me coming, because just before I got to the doorway he said, "Hey ki-, hey ki-" again. When I got there, I stopped. I couldn't help it, don't ask me why. I was stuck there, frozen like my feet were in cement. My eyes slid over to the left. The room was all white and big. Tiles covered the floor and walls. On the far end was a big cast iron tub like old houses still had. To the right was a toilet and this guy was sitting on it. He had a white gown on pushed up over his ass, and he was wearing white slippers. His head looked like an egg, lopsided and white, not a stitch of hair was on it.

"Hey ki-" he said, staring at me. He sounded like a moron. "No paipa, no paipa, ain't go no paipa, no tole paipa, no tole paipa!" He slurred real bad. "Err! err!-" he kept grunting like he had to take a shit but couldn't.

But there was a bad stink coming from in there. I shot ahead and bolted down the steps two at a time and ran into the living room all out of breath.

"What's the matter, Daniel?" the old bag asked.

"I, I, there's some guy up there in the bathroom. He says he ain't got no toilet paper I think he's trying to say." And I wanted to add I wasn't going by that damned door another six times, not for nothing.

"Oh, that's nothing," she said.

Nothing? What the hell did she mean by that?

"You see, that's my brother, Peter. He's slow."

"You mean he's a retard?" I asked.

"Well, yes he is mentally retarded, yes."

"He's the guy in that picture up there, isn't he-" I let slip out.

"Picture? Oh, I see you did some exploring, Daniel," she said.

"I didn't mean to-"

"It's quite alright. Yes, that's Peter."

I sat down. I was suddenly feeling real tired, like I'd been running a marathon or something. "Doesn't he need toilet paper?" I asked.

"He *never* needs toilet paper."

"He doesn't? How can that be? He made an awful stink up there," I said.

"That's only gas, I assure you. He doesn't go like most of us do. He only pretends. He wants to appear normal that way."

I didn't know what the hell she was talking about, and I didn't know why the hell I should care. I just knew I wanted to get off the subject real fast.

"What did you think of those pictures, Daniel?"

"Think of them? I don't know what you mean."

I know what you're thinking," she said with this sly kind of look on her face. She took a sip of her tea. The broad was trying to get into my head. "You're wondering how it could be that such a good looking young woman could end up looking like this."

How the hell could she have known that?

"It's natural for a man of your young age to think it, I assure you. Your mother, she's a very beautiful lady now, isn't   she?"

My throat was beginning to dry up and I squirmed a bit.

"Are you worried she'll end up looking like me someday? Is that what you're afraid of?"

"Look here," I said. "I never thought of any of that."

"Why don't you go upstairs and get the other three boxes," she said.

"What about your brother?" I asked.

"Just ignore him. He sits there like that much of the day."

Holy Christ, imagine that, sitting on the john all day, not being able to take a shit. I was really getting the creeps about this place.

I went back upstairs and practically ran past the goddamn bathroom and left the "Hey ki-" behind me when I ran right into a guy coming out from the next room down the hall.

"Christ!" I screamed. I jumped back and I swear my heart flipped out of my throat onto the floor. The guy had to be three times my size, and he was just a big black shape since the light was so shitty. My legs wouldn't work. I was stuck again.

"What can I do for you?" the guy asked. His voice was so deep it sounded like a tuba.

"I, uh, Mrs. Sweet wanted me to get stuff down from the attic."

"Oh yeah, let me help you with that," he said. "Name's Burger, Oscar," and he stuck out what must be the biggest damn hand on the planet. I stuck mine out and he swallowed it with his.

"After you," the tuba said. I figured it was all over. He'd close the door behind us and murder me, and no one would ever find my body. Ted had almost gotten it right. It wasn't a shitty thing I'd done last night, it was stupid, and I was going to die for it. But it was all Kowalski's fault.

The big guy followed me up the stairs. "Here, you take one box, I'll take the other two."

"What's with that guy on the shitter?" I asked, just trying to be friendly like. Maybe then he'd think I was an all right guy and wouldn't murder me after all.

The laugh that came from this guy sounded like it was from a really big tuba, it was so deep. "Oh don't mind old Pete. I'm his nurse."

"You're a nurse?" I thought all nurses were great looking broads.

"Well sort of. I take care of both Pete and Liz."

"Who's she?"

"Mrs. Sweet. I've known them two practically my whole life. She's one fine lady. After her husband passed away, I told her I'd take care of the both of them if she kept me on."

We went back down to the living room.

"Oh thank you Oscar, you didn't have to do that," Mrs. Sweet said.

"It's no problem," he said and left. Like he had a full schedule or something, what with his friend upstairs sitting on the stupid toilet all day.

So there I was, sitting in the middle of this dark stinking place with this old bag next to me, a stuffed dead

guy behind me, Frankenstein who sounded like a tuba, and a
retard who couldn't take a shit. What a fine way to spend a
Sunday. The front door seemed a million miles away. I don't
know what kept me from bolting right then and there, I
really don't.

"Did you know Daniel, that your father wanted to
become a doctor since the earliest age," Mrs. Sweet said.

"No kidding," I said.

"He could have been one, he certainly is smart
enough," she added.

"Why didn't he then?" I asked.

"He thought he ran out of time. You see your father
and mother got married and then the war came, and you two
children. Don't give up on your dreams, Daniel, ever. But
your father's done alright by himself."

"Yeah," I agreed. "I guess he could've done worse
than own a bowling alley."

"You're not proud of your father, are you?"

"Hey look, he my dad. It's not for me to say he
should've done differently. I guess some guys don't even
have a job. I just wish my mom didn't have to work there,
you know what I mean?"

"Your mother loves your father just the same as if he
was a doctor because he's a good family man. That's what
matters."

"What's in them boxes anyhow?" I asked.

"Bring me that one, there," she pointed. "Put it here
on the table."

I plopped it down in front of her. She began to take
out some crap, old military stuff, a uniform and medals, even
a gas mask.

"These are my husband's from the first World War. What do you think of them?"

"It's swell," I said. What the hell else was I to say? I felt like all of a sudden her dead husband would come out from behind the curtain and put it all on.

"Your father was a war hero also, just like Mr. Sweet."

"Yeah, I heard. But I've never heard him talk about it."

"No real hero will ever talk about what made them a hero, remember that," she said.

What the hell was she getting at, I thought. Then she said, "Hero's uniforms come in all types. Here give me the other box there."

I took the first one away after she put the stuff back in it, and brought the second one to her.

"The reason I wanted you to come over was to see what is in the next three boxes. But I wanted to show you the first one also."

I stifled a yawn.

"These last three are my husband's collection."

More boring war shit, I figured. She opened the second box. Before I tell you what was in it, and the other two, I have to tell you something about myself. I've got to be the biggest Yankee fanatic in the whole world. I'll consider my life worthwhile if I could just get to a Series game at the Stadium. Just one. She unfolded a uniform with the Yankee NY on it. Then she brought out signed baseballs and cards, and from the other two boxes more cards and photos and even a glove.

"I can't remember whose uniform this was," she said. But I knew it had to be Yogi's or Mize's since it had an eight on the back.

"How did he get all of this?" I asked.

""Mr. Sweet and I used to take on boarders from the Yankee club. And we would travel to Florida to see them play down there. Mr. Sweet was very good friends with many of them. Another reason why I wanted you to come over here was to hear stories I can tell you, stories about what went on in this very house with those boys."

In one minute, the worst day of my life had turned into something I couldn't have imagined, and a stuffy old place had turned into the Hall of Fame, and an old bag had turned into the best friend a guy could ever have.

"Did any of them sit on this chair, with these sheets on them even?" I asked.

"Well sure they did, but I can't recall whether these covers were on them or not," she answered.

"Did your brother Pete know any of them?"

"No, he wasn't with us then."

I was glad. I couldn't imagine DiMaggio and the rest of them having to put up with a retard.

"Would you like to hear some of those stories now?" she asked.

She talked all day and into the night, and I looked at the pictures over and over again, and she told stories of Florida even. I remember we ate and drank, but Oscar Frankenstein brought them to us right there in the living room so we wouldn't get interrupted. And then the damndest thing happened. She stood up and said, "I almost forgot! I can't miss him!" She got all animated like. She went over to the curtains and opened them up. Instead of a dead guy behind them there was a T.V. set. I was a little disappointed it wasn't her husband, because maybe he could have come back to life to tell me some stories too.

"You've got a television set?" I asked stupidly. "We used to have one, but we had to keep taking it back so we gave up."

She turned it on, and she got lucky, because whom she wanted to see came right on. It was that Elvis guy on the Ed Sullivan show again. I'd seen him once before. I didn't think much of him or his music. He danced like some fag, if you ask me. But she loved him, just like all the damn chicks did. And she started dancing, trying to imitate him. Imagine that. I think she even started to look like the person in the picture upstairs, I swear. And then she looked at me while she was dancing, all out of breath, and she said, "I want you to have all of it, my husband's baseball collection, I mean. I know how much it would mean to you. Your mother has discussed with me what a great fan you are of the boys."

Imagine that.

3

The way I got it figured, I was already doomed. You see, everybody's old man and old lady's got one of two attitudes about us kids. Either we were "really going places," or we'd "never amount to anything." How they could be so damn cocksure about it beat the hell out of me, but they were.

Take my brother and me, for instance. Ted was in the "really going places" category. He a genius, everybody's always saying. He's a dreamer, always reading up on this and that, doing all kinds of scientific experiments and shit. Our bedroom's got this bookcase in it and there must be a thousand books and magazines on it, crap like 'I, Robot', and 'Galaxy', and 'Astounding Science Fiction', 'Amazing Stories' and whatnot. He's got books by those guys Asimov and Clarke and Heinlein.

He's always impressing the hell out of my old man like at dinner table conversations. "Hey dad," he'll say, "Mr. Clarke says in the near future we're going to have satellites orbiting the earth, in geosynchronous orbit!"

"What geosynchronous?" my mother would ask, saving the old man from the embarrassment of having to ask it. Like anybody else on the planet except Ted and this Clarke jerk knew what the hell it meant.

"Well," he proceeded to say, "You see, geosynchronous means these satellites will be such a height above the earth that their orbit will exactly coincide with the earth's spin, and so be stationary with respect to it."

"So what the hell's with that," I asked. "I mean so what-"

But you see I got cut off. "Danny, let Ted finish!" the old man said.

"Well, imagine those satellites will be positioned all around the earth. Then we will be able to beam television and radio signals off of them. That means that anywhere on earth, people will be able to receive a signal from anyone else almost simultaneously. We'll be able to watch events from all over the world, live!"

"That sounds very exciting, Ted!" my mom said.

That sounds like total bullshit, I want to say. "Hey, have I told you guys what I did today in school?" I said lamely.

"How will these satellites get in orbit, Ted?" the old man asked, totally ignoring me.

"Rockets, dad. Dr. Werner Von Braun is leading the technology. He came to our country during the war. Our Vanguard program will someday put a man in space. We'll soon be in the Space Age, instead of the Atomic Age."

"I'm going to do a project for the science fair!" I blurted out.

"Vanguard program, huh?" the old man said, further ignoring me.

"Henry. I think Daniel is trying to tell us something, aren't you dear?" the old lady said.

Ted looked at me. "What was that you said?"

"I said that I'm going to do a project for the science fair."

"You? That's a laugh!" good old Ted said.

"Now Ted! Daniel is allowed to, now. I think that's a wonderful idea, Daniel," my old lady said.

"What. What's your project?" Ted said snotly.

Of course I had no idea what project I was going to do, especially since I'd had no idea I was going to do one until just a few moments ago when I made the story up. I wasn't even sure there *was* a stupid science fair anymore. I just vaguely remember Ted always starting his around now. "I haven't finished thinking about it yet." I said.

"You don't know a damn thing about science, you moron." Ted said.

"Teddy!" the old lady yelled. "That kind of talk is uncalled for!"

I was going to have to think of something, eventually, of course. There was no going back. I was going to have to show that science freak of a brother of mine a thing or two of what Danny McTavish was capable of doing when he put his mind really to it. Hell, I know I'm not a brain, not in a scholastic way, but I got a lot of sense. Something he doesn't have. I was going to have to show him up.

Yup, I had to show him up, even if I was a kid who'd never amount to anything.

I decided to hold a meeting with the boys. It had to be top secret, so as to make sure no snoopy parents or brothers or sisters could listen in. I decided to have it down at the ball field. I waited for them to show up, sitting on the pitcher's mound early Saturday morning. We had to get an early start.

A few minutes later the boys showed up on their bikes.

"This had better be good," Lance said. "I'm missin' bottle cap baseball, you know."

"Yeah, yeah, it's good. It's important," I said.

"Hey buddy," Jerry said. "Did you hear about kid Kowalski?"

"Kowalski's kid?" I said. "What?"

"Well, since everybody in town heard about your antics of Saturday night, word somehow spread to his old lady that his old man had the kid fillin' in at the lanes."

"So?" I asked.

"So she came to school and took the kid away."

"Well, there you are," I said. "Not only was I right about him foulin', I did the kid a service. He's got to be better off with her than with that freak of an old man of his."

"So what're we here for?" Lance asked.

I reached into my pocket and fished out two cards, both signed by Johnny Mize.

"Hey thanks!" Lance said, sticking his paw out.

"Uh uh," I said. "You ain't takin' nuthin' till we complete the mission."

"You're up to somethin' Danny boy, what's it this time?" Jerry asked.

"We're going to do a project for the science fair," I said.

"Science fair?" Lance said. It sounded like he didn't believe me.

"Yeah, science fair," I said.

"Us?" Lance asked.

"Yeah, us," I said.

"We don't do science fairs," Lance said. "Guys like your brother do that kinda' shit. What's up?"

"I gotta' show up Ted, that's what's up," I said. "I just do."

"Ted's in high school, a junior, " Jerry said. "He doesn't do science fairs anymore."

"Yeah, but so what? I still have to do one. Except we gotta' make it look like I did it myself."

"If it's any good, no one will believe you did it yourself, you know that Danny," Lance said. "You know us two ain't no help, anyway."

Then a big grin grew on Jerry's face. "I know why you gotta do this," he said.

"I already told you why," I said.

"Nah, that ain't the real reason," he said. "What the hell you care what Ted thinks of you?"

"It ain't just him," I said. "It's the old man I really will show up. He thinks Ted's the know it all, you know. Especially since it looks like he'll be goin' to Princeton."

"Princeton?" Lance said. "He's gonna skip his senior yeahr?"

"Nah, I think they're just draftin' him or somethin'. You know, he did some kinda' crap there already, so they want to make sure he doesn't go anywhere else."

I ain't ever heard of no school drafting anybody," Jerry said. "Sounds screwy to me. Anyway, I know why you really want to do it."

"Huh."

"It's 'cause of Tina," he said.

"Tina?"

"Yeah, Tina. You got the hots for her."

"She's got the hots for *me*, you mean," I said. "I don't need any help in the babe department from doing a stupid science fair project. You're off your rocker."

That was one thing I had over Ted. And that was the ladies. They loved me, and I was smooth as silk with them. While other guys stammered, afraid to ask the best looking girls out, me, I never was afraid to ask any girl out. The prettier the more suave I was. Yeah, that was one thing I had over my genius brother. If he ever got married it would be to some cow who read the same crap he did. When we grew up I'd be parading around with some gorgeous chick, and he'd have some squat four-eyed dame bossin' him around on a leash. And maybe then he'd wake up to there being real women in the world, and he'd be hanging his tongue out looking at mine all day.

Hey, if I did as good as the old man did, I'd have done ok in my book.

Old Ted, I hoped he made it real big in the outer space department, I really did. They made those phony looking Buck Rogers type of movies, with the guys in space suits and all and he really dug that shit. Me, I'll stick to terra firma, as they say.

"I'll help you if you let me use that lifetime pass you got," Lance said.

"No way, you'll lose it," I said. What he was talking about, was, I found in the bottom of one of the boxes with the baseball stuff in it, a small fancy looking felt box, and inside was a big gold coin. On one side was engraved the facade at the Stadium. On the other it said Twenty-Fifth anniversary and Lifetime Pass. It was dated nineteen forty-seven. Sometime I had to ask old lady Sweet if she knew whose pass it had been.

"How am I gonna lose it?" Lance began to argue. "It's too big to lose. I ain't gonna confuse it with no quarter or nuthin'."

"Forget it," I said. "Nobody uses it except me."

"All that stuff she gave you must be worth a fortune, huh Danny?" Jerry said. "Couple hundred bucks, maybe."

"Gotta be more than that," I said. "Look, you use the pass say in the box seat, that's worth, what, how much are box seats?"

"Three fifty I think," Lance said.

"Who says you get a box seat you use that thing?" Jerry said.

"Well, the dough will add up fast, you use it every day."

"Maybe if you show them the pass, we can all get in," Lance said.

"You crazy?" I said. "You think they're going to let you fill up the whole stadium with your friends with one pass?"

"How 'bout that glove you got.' That's worth somethin'," Jerry said.

"Yeah," I said. "Anyway, we're here for the science fair. You guys got any ideas?"

"You're lucky Danny," Lance said.

"What?"

"That Tina, she's hot."

"Yeah, well, don't get any funny ideas about stealin' my chick," I said, kidding like. Lance wasn't too strong in the chick department, like I was.

"She grow any tities yet?" Or is they all falsies?" Jerry asked. "Huh?" he smiled.

"He ain't gonna tell us," Lance said.

"That's 'cause he doesn't know" Jerry said.

"Yeah, they're there all right," I said. "I told her she didn't have to wear no falsies."

"Yeah, really?" Lance said.

"Sure, sure I did."

"How far you get with her, I mean so far?" Jerry asked with that stupid grin on his stupid face.

"It's going, going, gone, a home run! like Mel Allen says, huh Danny, fess up," Lance said.

Sometimes I try to have serious conversations with people, but it never works out.

"You hit for the cycle, didn't ya?" Jerry said.

"Look, guys-" I said. "What about-"

"I don't think Tina's the kind of girl who'd go there, do you think, Danny?" Lance asked. "Not with *her* old man."

"What, what are you talking about?" I asked, panicking. "How do you know about him?"

"Well, c'mon, no guinea old man's gonna let some punk like you score real big with his daughter. He'd put a contract on your ass if he didn't kill you himself."

"Yeah, I guess. But I'm not worried about it. First base is all I got, well maybe second."

So you had a two bagger then, is about you're sayin'," Jerry said.

"I didn't-"

"That's not bad," he said.

"Better'n us, huh Jerr" Lance said.

Before I go on, I'd better tell you about the time after I'd just met Tina. Yeah she was good looking all right. I'd been eyeing her something fierce at school. She was just my type. Kind of cute and sexy at the same time. As good as I am with the girls, I really didn't expect to have much of a shot makin' the move, you know, inviting her to a dance and all that kind of crap, not with older guys from high school making moves on her too. But I guess I had underestimated the power of my charisma, because she asked *me* out. We started hanging out together, and I walked her home from school a couple of times. Then we made a date like to meet at the next dance. So we ended up dancing, doing that new rock and roll crap, which I really don't like, especially from that Elvis guy, like I was saying before. We hit if off real good. So the next week she came up to me in school and said that I should come over to meet her parents, say Friday. What for do I have to meet them, I asked stupidly, and she said it was because she liked me, and wanted to show me off kind of like. Well, it turned out her parents had to go out of town for a few days, so when I came over we kind of messed around after her grandmother, who was watching, her had fallen asleep.

Anyway, the next Friday I made it over to her house again. She even invited me for dinner. So first we went into her living room and sat down on this love seat so we were pretty damn close to one another. I was dressed nice like I was going to church. Tina was all dolled up, too. So then her parents came downstairs. I stood up and got introduced to them, and they sat down on a big sofa across from us.

I swear to God, I'd never seen anything like it, her old lady, I mean. Think of Tina but magnified a million times over, in the beauty department, that is. She had on one of them short dresses around her knees, and when she sat down it kind of crept up over them, and I got a pretty good peek at her thighs just before she smoothed her dress like the ladies do. I think I started to sweat real bad because it felt like I was squirting under my armpits, and my shirt started sticking to my body. I remember thinking holy cow, is Tina's breasts going to grow like that? I knew she'd never have the face this broad had. Tina had too much of her old man in her. I know about such things, believe me.

Sometime during the conversations, her old lady leaned forward and grabbed a bowl of nuts on the table between us and offered them to me. I got a bitty look at some delicious cleavage. I spied her hands as she gave me the bowl, and they looked like one of them mannequins, long and real smooth, pearly like. I tried not to look at her face too much, except when she was talking to me, of course. I'm tellin' you, you've never seen a face like this, trust me. Let's just say she's some sort of goddess. And she had on a pearl necklace, which blended like into that skin of hers, they looked so much alike with that sheen and all.

I don't know who said what, really, I was on cloud nine, to tell the truth. I think I remember mumbling stuff. When we got up to eat, I ended up sitting across from Tina, with her parents at the ends. By then, Tina looked like some little punk kid with falsies. Which I guess you could say she is.

But here's why I panicked when Lance said something about Tina's old man putting a contract out on me. You see, when we finished eating, Tina's old man said he wanted to speak to me out on the porch. I figured it would be a good man-to-man talk sort of thing, about what a nice clean cut young man I was, and it was alright by him if Tina and I were an item, and that sort of bullshit. But it didn't exactly turn out that way. We made it to the porch all right, and the next thing I know the big guy is poking me with his fat finger into my chest, and it hurts like hell but I stood my ground, and he's going on about how he never wants me to see his lousy daughter again, and the things he'd do to me if I didn't follow his orders. I think he said I was a pervert because of the way I was so obviously hitting on his wife. It was a stupid use of the word, if you ask me, just because I had the hots for his wife. I knew he was a guinea wop kind of person so I kind of did get scared, to tell the truth. He told me to beat it and not come back, which I of course didn't. So what Lance and Jerry hadn't figured out yet was that Tina and me were no longer an item. And this had happened a few weeks ago.

"What's your secret anyway, lover boy?" Jerry asked.

"Secret? What secret?" I asked.

"Ya know, with the ladies."

"Ain't no secret," I said. "You act like it's a secret and no dame'll go for you. You gotta advertise yourself, say what's on your mind, that's all."

I once tried that," Lance said. "It didn't do me any good."

"Who with?" I asked.

"That girl Holly," he said, kind of embarrassed, I could tell.

"Holly Atkins? In seventh grade?" I asked.

"Yeah, that's her."

She ain't too good looking there Lance," Jerry said.

"Yeah, well, I figured I'd practice on her."

"What'd she say?" I asked. "You ask her out or something?"

"Nah. Nuthin' like that."

"What then?"

"I asked her if I could walk her home."

"That's it?" Jerry asked. "So what'd she say?"

"She told me to beat it. She said I was a creep and a loser hangin' out with the likes of you guys."

"You're making that up," I said.

"Yeah, she did, I swear, and she mentioned you specifically."

"What did I do? She doesn't even know me."

"Everybody knows you, Danny," Lance said. "All the crazy things you do."

"That ain't true."

"Yeah, well *she* does. She even mentioned you and Tina are history."

"What? She said that? How would she know that?"

"I guess word's gotten around how you pissed off Tina's old man."

"What?" I said. This was turning into a goddamned nightmare, this Tina thing, and I'd only been going with her a couple of weeks. Her old man was ready to send the goon squad after me. "Why didn't you tell me about this before for Christ's sake?"

"I figured you knew. What'd you do?"

"I didn't know this shit was in the newspapers practically!"

"What's he talkin' about now, Danny boy?" Jerry asked.

"Nuthin'," I said.

"How the hell you piss off Tina's old man with what, one visit?" Jerry asked.

"Yeah, how'd you manage to do that, lover boy?" Lance asked.

"I kind of looked at her old lady funny."

"What's that mean?" Lance asked.

"Well, she ain't too bad looking and-"

"Christ, what'd you do, make a move on her?" Lance asked.

"No, you think I'm crazy?"

"You went ahead and spoiled it for the rest of us," Lance said. "No girl's gonna talk to any of us mutts now. You went and gave us all a bad rap."

"I didn't make a move on her," I said. "Her old man was sitting right next to her, and Tina was next to me."

"Yeah, and?" Jerry asked.

"So, anyway, I kind of looked her over. She's gorgeous. You ever seen her? No, that's what I thought. So don't make any judgements. How'd you like it if you're sitting there, all stuffy like, next to your goddamned girlfriend, and her old lady with this skirt on sits across from you and she makes her daughter look like a goddamn kid with no tits, and she then she bends over and all that shit."

"I'd like it real fine," Jerry said.

"Yeah, well, you weren't there, so you didn't have to put up with it, fallin' in love right then and there, but there's not a goddamn thing you can do about it but squirm and sweat. I felt about two years old."

"You think Tina's gonna look like her old lady some day? Jerry asked. "Man, I oughta see if I can charm her someway, even if you did ruin it for all of us. When I come over to her house I'll act like a gentleman, not a pervert like you."

"Pervert? That's what her old man said I was. How's me lookin' at his wife make me a pervert?"

"It's entirely inappropriate behavior," Jerry said.

"Up yours," I said. "And she's not going to look too much like her old lady, on account of she's got too much of her old man in her, you ask my opinion. I can't believe that little shit ratted on me, that even her old man would tell her that. What's the world coming to anyway when a guy can't even look at a broad?"

"Did you drool, even, huh Danny?" Jerry asked.

"Screw off," I said.

"So he kicked you out?" Lance asked.

"Yeah, he took me out on the porch and started jabbin' me in the chest like this-"

"Hey!"

"-and called me a pervert. He told me if I ever saw his dumb ass daughter again he'd kill me or something."

"Yeah, everybody knows that," Lance said.

"*You* did, you punk, but you didn't tell me 'til just now. Come to think of it, Tina's been doing a good job of staying away from me, giving me rotten looks. Guess I should've known her old man had told her what was going on."

The three of us shot the shit a while longer, and then they said they had to go. It was then I remembered the two cards stuck in my back pocket. I guess the guys figured they weren't worth doing any stupid science fair project for.

4

That's ok; I didn't need them anyway. I had a great idea. You see, I started looking at those magazines Ted was always reading. I read about futuristic bull crap. I read about rockets sending stuff into space, into orbit around the earth, without falling right back down. I didn't get how that could happen, I mean with gravity and all. But I really got into that satellite bullshit and kind of dug it. If I wanted to show the old man and Ted up, I had to do something with them satellites.

And then I got a really good idea. Ted had been going to Princeton the past few summers doing some sort of scientific bullshit. So I figured I could pay them a visit, maybe even to the same guy he went to, some professor or whatever to help me out. I'd found out from the science teacher, Mr. Jacobs, that the science fair was in three weeks, but that it was too late to sign up. And he pretty much laughed when I told him I wanted to do one.

"*You* want to participate in the science fair McTavish?" the goon asked like the snot he is.

"Yeah, why not?" I said.

"You don't have any interest in the subject whatsoever, so why start now? The only reason why I didn't flunk you last semester was because of your brother, to tell the truth."

"My brother? What's he got to do with it?"

"Well, you were borderline. Your grade could have gone either way."

"Yeah, so?"

"So Ted was the best student I've ever had in twenty years of teaching. He is going places, and you're not. So I couldn't see the reasoning in flunking you. I didn't want to embarrass Ted or your parents. I figured I owed Ted that. And I certainly didn't want to have you again in my class."

"Am I flunking this semester?" I asked.

I believe so, yes."

"Well, I'll make you a deal," I said.

"I don't make deals with students, McTavish."

"Let me do a project, and if I don't have the winning project, fail me. If I do, then pass me."

"How could you possibly have the best project, as long as you have something to do with it?" the creep asked.

"I've been reading up on things. I'm close to picking one."

"I'll give you two days to come up with one."

"Three. That'll give me until Monday."

"Yes, then, three. But you have to tell me something, McTavish."

"What's that sir?"

"How come Tina Roma hates your guts now?"

"She does?" I asked. What is the whole goddamned world in on this?

"Anyone can see," he said. "What did you do now, McTavish? You alienate people constantly, don't you? If it wasn't for your friends Lance and Jerry, you wouldn't have any. Why do you think that is?"

I wanted to tell him it was because most everybody was a goon like him, but I said, "Can't say, Mr. Jacobs. Like you said, I'm not going places, so what difference does it make?"

"Monday, McTavish. Come up with something decent."

"Yes sir, thanks for the opportunity."

So on Saturday morning I hitchhiked to Princeton. I'd told the old lady I was going out with the guys to play some ball.

I'd rummaged through Ted's project stuff to find out what professor he'd worked with over there. He'd done projects on some sort of propulsion thing, something about cars of the future. It seemed like nobody worked on present stuff; it was always future shit. I found the guy's name all right.

I ended up in the administration building and asked some broad there where I could find the professor, a guy by the name of Wheeling.

"Professor Wheeling's office is in the Science Building on Olden Street. But he's not here on campus today. He's home. What is the nature of your business, young man?" she asked.

" I need his help with a project," I said.

"Are you a student here at Princeton University?" she asked. One thing I hate is a smart ass.

"Well, no, not exactly, but-"

"Then I'm sorry, I can't help you."

"Look, see, my brother Ted, Ted McTavish, he's a friend of the professor. He's done some projects with him," I said.

"Oh, so your brother is a student here?"

"No, he did some summer projects. Look, I just need to see the guy, it's important."

"You'll have to wait until Monday, I'm sorry."

"I can't wait until Monday."

"And I don't imagine the professor has time to see a child, anyway."

The bitch was really getting on my nerves.

"Ok, ok, I get it," I said. I stormed off. I'd have to do it the hard way. Fortunately I remembered the guy's first name was Larry, so I went to a phone booth. I looked him up and got the address. There was a map in the book, which I tore out. He lived close by.

I located the apartment and rang the bell. The door opened, and a tall skinny guy answered.

"Yes?" he said.

"Hi, I'm looking for the professor."

"Yes?"

"Hi, Mr. Larry Wheeling?"

"*Dr.* Lawrence Wheeling." He had a pipe and stuck it in his mouth. He seemed either amused or pissed off, I couldn't tell which. The smell of tobacco was so thick it hit me like a wall. He blew a big trail of smoke over my head. "Well?"

"I, uh, I wanted to know if you could help me," I said.

"Are you lost?" he asked.

"Not now, I found you."

"Well then, what is it?" he asked. He wasn't much on conversation.

"My name's Daniel McTavish. You know my brother Ted, he's-"

"Yes, I know who your brother is. Don't tell me you're even more brilliant then him, and wish to attend the University already?"

He put a little smile on his face, and I wanted to smack him.

"No, nothing like that. But I was wondering if you could help me with a science project."

"How did you get here?" he asked, and looked over my head, looking for a car, I guess.

"I hitchhiked."

"Quite adventurous aren't you?"

"Yeah, I guess you could say that," I agreed.

"All right, come in."

I entered a living room. There were books everywhere, on the couch, on a chair, on a big table, on the walls. Some were open. The place was messed with books. I could see a kitchen and a bedroom through the other side. It was a small place. It didn't look like smart guys made too much dough.

"What can I get you, Ted's brother? You must have need of a drink, no?"

I hadn't realized how thirsty I was until he'd brought up the subject.

"Yeah, thanks, water's fine."

He went into the kitchen, so I got a chance to look around. And I hit the jackpot. I noticed something, which might prove real useful.

He handed me a glass. "So tell me, you are a budding scientist like your brother, I take it?"

I figured I might as well go along with it so I lied, "Yeah, I've been reading up on satellites."

"Satellites?"

"Yeah, how we're going from the Atomic Age into the Space Age soon. How we're going to put satellites around the earth, and send signals off of them."

"Quite possibly, yes," he said. "It's nice to see someone like yourself is so interested in science and technology. How old are you, son?"

"Fourteen. Two years younger than Ted."

"I see."

"So, anyway," I said, "I came here to see if you could help me in a project for a science fair. I'd like to do it on those satellites. You know, show the earth with the satellites all around it, stuck in orbit like Ted, or like Mr. Clarke said would happen.

"Help you? Why would you need the assistance of a professor? Anyone can do such a thing. Just make some balls out of clay, or plaster, or some such, as you children do. I'm much too busy."

"No, no, I thought we could make it electric like, with signals beaming up to the satellites, make it look real."

"Daniel, really, I have more important things to do with my time. Look at all these books. There is never enough time."

"I see you're a Yankee fan, professor."

"How's that?" he asked.

"I noticed the cap there. It's signed?"

"Why, yes."

"I'll make you a deal. I've got a signed uniform of Johnny Mize you can have if you help me."

"Whom does it belong to, really?"

"It's mine, really. An old lady gave it to me along with a bunch of other stuff," I said but shouldn't have.

"Really?" Like what?" he asked.

"I'll throw in an autographed card of Joe DiMaggio's.

"Really!" He started puffing real hard on his stinking pipe. I almost gagged. "When is this project due?"

"I got three weeks," I said.

"All right, we'll work the next two weekends. I'll think on it. Come back early next Saturday, say nine o'clock."

"You got it, professor. Thanks a lot!" I said and headed home.

When I returned the next Saturday, a note was taped to the door,

'McTavish, go to the Graduate College over on College Road. Just ask for Sam and Barry Goldstein and you'll be directed to their room. They are expecting you.'

I didn't know what this was all about, and it took me almost an hour to find the place. I asked around, and finally someone told me what room they lived in. What the hell? Why couldn't the professor have met me?

I knocked on an open door.

"Yes?" I heard.

"Hi, can I come in?" I asked.

"You McTavish?" the voice asked.

"Yeah," I said.

"Come on in," the voice said.

I swung the door open some more. Two guys were sitting at a table, and it was like I was looking at a reflection. They both looked the same.

"Hey, come on in," one of the two said. He got up and stuck out his hand. "I'm Barry, this is my brother Sam."

"Hey," I said

"We're graduate assistants of Professor Wheeling's," Barry said. "He told us about a science fair project you wanted to do. He said for us to work on it. You a friend of his, or something?"

"Well, sort of."

"Well, you made a hell of an impression on him, I can tell you that. The professor told us to help you, without actually ordering us to, if you know what I mean. What's so important about a science fair project, we've been asking ourselves."

"Sure have," his brother said.

"Did he tell you what I'd like to do it on?"

"No," Sam said.

"Well, I've been reading up on satellites, about how this Clarke guy says pretty soon they'll be all over the place, and we'll be beaming signals off them."

"You a member of the Relay League?" Barry asked.

"What's that?" I asked.

"You know, the American Radio Relay League," he said.

"Ain't never heard of it," I said.

"Well, you'll have to become a member, man," Barry said. I was getting in way over my head. I was mixing it up with the wrong crowd.

"You've got a radio, right?" Sam asked.

"Yeah, sure," I said. "Just like any guy."

"What's your handle?" Sam asked.

"It doesn't have a handle. It's real small."

"Small?"

"Yeah."

"What model you have?"

I shrugged. "Look, I use it to listen to ballgames, music, you know."

"Ballgames?" Barry said. "Don't you ever talk to anyone?"

"Talk?" I asked. "I thought radios were for listening."

"You *do* have a ham radio, right?" Sam asked.

"Ham?" I asked. What the hell were these two squares talking about? They were really getting on my nerves.

"Yeah, a ham" Tweedledee said.

"Sam," Tweedledum said. "It obvious Danny doesn't know what we're talking about. Danny, you want to do a project about satellite communication, but you don't know what a ham radio is?"

"So? Anyway, I've got an idea about it."

"What's that?" Tweedledee asked.

I told them my idea of using blinking lights showing the signal bouncing around the world like I saw in the magazine.

"Not bad," Tweedledum said. "But we could build you a replica of the Vanguard satellite we're going to send up, instead. We just read an article in 'Discover the Stars' about how to make it."

"That's no good," I said. "I already told my science teacher what I was going to do the project on."

"Well, look Danny," Tweedledee said, "If you're into the future of satellite communication, you've got to learn about ham radio. What do you say, Sam, we show him the club?"

"Yeah, we'll show him the club," Tweedledum agreed.

"Club? What club?" I asked.

"Our ham radio club," he said.

"Look, I need to think about getting back home. You guys going to do the project?" I asked.

"Yeah, we'll do it," Tweedledum said. "Wheeling didn't give us a choice. We'll give you a ride home, how's that? That'll give you a bunch of time."

"Yeah, a bunch of time," Tweedledee agreed.

The club was downstairs in a basement. All these gadgets were set up on tables. They had dials but they didn't look anything like my radio at home.

"Pretty cool, huh?" Tweedledum asked.

"Yeah, real cool," I agreed

"You see you dial the frequency you want to talk and listen with. See, this thing is the mike. You push this button here on the side to talk, let go to listen. We talk to people from all over the world," Tweedledee pointed out.

"Why would anybody want to do that?" I asked.

"Why not?" he answered.

"I don't know," I shrugged.

"You ought to know for your project that the world community of scientists has planned the IGY, the

International Geophysical Yeahr to study the earth. It's starting soon, right Sam?"

"That's right, in July!" Tweedledum said.

"And as part of it, the United States is going to launch a satellite as a result of the Vanguard program," Tweedledee said.

"It's the year of maximum sun spot activity," Tweedledum said. "The satellite will be a unique laboratory from which to observe the sun and the earth."

"That is, if the commies don't beat us to it, right Barry?" Tweedledum said.

"Yeah, that's a laugh," Tweedledee said and laughed.

"A laugh?" I asked, totally lost. "Why is it a laugh?"

"They can't even build refrigerators," Tweedledum said.

"They're bigger than us though," I said.

"Bigger?" Tweedledee asked.

"Well, ya know, if you look on a map, the Russkies country is a lot bigger than ours. They must have a lot of people there and they must be good for something. I mean if we can do it, why couldn't they?"

"Haven't you learned anything at school Danny?" Tweedledum asked. "The commies are all screwed up on account of their commies. They've had some top notch scientists, everybody knows that, but nobody listens to them over there."

"Look at this Danny," Tweedledee said. "This is an 0457Z military surplus recorder, and this is a receiver. We'll be ready to pick up and receive the signal from our satellite next yeahr. The frequency decided on will be one o eight megacycles."

"You don't say," I said.

"Danny, what's in this science project for the professor? What's this all about, anyway?" Tweedledum asked.

"Oh, a family thing," I said.

"So anyway, we'll have this thing ready for you next weekend, ok?" Tweedledee said. "We'll come up with something. You'll win for sure."

"Great," I said.

"How far away do you live?" Tweedledum asked.

"Maybe five miles tops," I said.

"We'll drop it off at your house, and give you a call first, so give us your phone number."

"Sounds good," I said.

"I like your idea, Danny, It's good," Tweedledum said.

"Thanks."

"We'll use sequential lighting, right Barr?"

"Yup, sequential lighting. You got it."

"What are you guys studying in school anyway?" I asked.

"Physics. We're studying to be physicists. Tweedledee said. "You know what they do, right?"

"Some sort of physical thing, I guess, like phys ed?"

"Phys ed?"

"You know, like gym class," I said.

"Gym class?" Tweedledum said. "What the hell are you talking about, Danny?"

"Hell, I dunno, you tell me." These two guys were starting to drive me nuts, but I had to go along with them. They were going to make me a winner.

"Physicists study the laws of nature," Tweedledee said. "Propose theories, that sort of thing. Like Newton, he was a physicist, you've heard of him?"

"Yeah, I think we studied him," I said. If it wasn't for that bastard I wouldn't be flunking science, it seemed to me.

Just then a knock came at the door.

"Yeah," Tweedledee yelled.

The door opened and a guy came down the stairs.

"Hey Stevie," Tweedledee said.

"Hey guys," Stevie said.

Stevie had to be six five and looked to weigh about a hundred pounds, tops. He had a giant Adam's apple sticking out the front of his throat. His face was pretty pimpley. He reminded me of Bazooka Joe.

"Hey Stevie, this is Danny," Tweedledee said.

"Hey Danny," BJ said and stuck out his hand. It was real sweaty.

"Hi Stevie," I said.

"What's up?" BJ asked.

"Danny's family is a friend of Wheeling. He's asked us to help him with a science project. He didn't give us much of a choice, if you know what I mean."

"Yeah, he can be that way," BJ said.

BJ went over to one of the ham radios and flipped a switch. A low hum came out of it.

"What's up?" Tweedledum asked BJ.

"It's one o'clock. I told Brainstorm I'd give him a call."

BJ turned a dial so a number above it said twenty-eight. He picked up the microphone and said, "Brainstorm, this is Wonder Boy, come in, over."

"Wonder Boy, I'm here, over," came through the speaker.

"What's new, Brainstorm, over."

"Getting close to summer, looking forward to working on our project, over."

"Copy that, come up with any new ideas, over."

"Yeah, I'll show you next week, over."

Tweedledee grabbed the microphone from BJ and said, "Hey Brainstorm, Lucky Twin here. Feel like helping us out on a project, over?"

"What's that, over?"

"There's a kid here. Prof Wheeling told us to help out with his science project. The kid wants to do it on satellites, over."

"Satellites, over?"

"Yeah, it'll be pretty cool, actually. We're going to use sequential lights to simulate a beamed signal, you know, from base stations up to the satellites and down again. The kid thought of it, actually. Says he read about Clarke's ideas on it. Pretty sharp kid, I'd say, over."

"What's this kid look like?" Brainstorm asked.

"I dunno, what do you look like Danny?"

"Danny?" Brainstorm asked. "Danny, that you?"

Oh shit. I knew I recognized the voice. I put my finger to my mouth and shook my head. "No, no!" I whispered.

"Danny, you there?" Ted asked.

"You know this kid, Brainstorm, over?" Tweedledee fuckhead asked.

"Ask him if he's my stupid brother, over."

"You his brother?" Tweedledum asshole asked.

"Give me that thing," I said and grabbed the microphone. "Ted, you've got to-"

"Kid," BJ interrupted. "You've got to push the button to talk."

"Ted! You've got to keep quiet about this. Mom thinks I'm with the guys. My teacher can't know about any of this!"

"You idiot," Ted said. "You'll be in big trouble again, buddy."

"No! I'll be right home! Where'd you get one of these ham radios, anyway?"

"It's not mine, and don't change the subject."

"Please Ted, let me handle this," I begged.

"You're hopeless, Danny. I really don't give a shit. Do what you want. Why is Wheeler helping you, anyway? What the hell are you doing at Princeton?"

"He's a big Yankee fan, I found out."

"What? You're giving your precious stuff away?"

"Please Ted, just this one time, please don't say anything to anybody."

"You'll hang yourself in the end, you always do. Let me speak to Lucky Twin."

"Ok Ted."

Shit. Fuck. How the hell did this happen? You can't tell me my fate isn't to get fucked every time with everything. Coincidences like this just don't happen to everybody.

"Hey Brainstorm," Tweedledee said. "So your brother has baseball stuff he offered Wheeling if we help him, over?

"Sounds like it, over."

"Guess you aren't going to help. Actually, you should do the whole thing, he's your brother, over."

"You shouldn't help him," Ted said. "He won't get away with it. His teacher will see right through it, over."

"Yeah, I know what you mean. But maybe not. And we don't have any choice, over."

"Let me talk to Wonder Boy, over," Ted said.

Tweedledee gave the microphone back to BJ who started talking to Ted.

"Hey guys, you won't tell Wheeling you know about the baseball stuff, right?" I asked.

"Nah, don't worry about it," Tweedledee said.

"Nah, that would be shitty," Tweedledum said.

They took me home. I held my breath.

Of course Ted said something to me that night. At least he was decent enough not to mention it in front of the folks. In fact, I got a real scare when the old lady brought the whole thing up at the dinner table.

"So Daniel," she said. "How is it going with your science fair project?"

I kept my head down, staring into my plate. "Well, I've been working on it, actually," I mumbled.

"Really?" she said. "You're hardly ever around, and when you are, I don't see you working on it. I don't see anything."

"I'm working on it somewhere else."

"Somewhere else? What do you mean? Why would you need to work on it somewhere else?"

I could feel Ted's brain boring into mine. I kept waiting for him to say something, but he didn't. I had to say something quick, so he wouldn't feel he had to.

"Actually, the guys are helping me out. It's kind of big. You know, six hands are better than two kind of a thing."

"But this is *your* project, right Daniel? The spirit of the science fair is to show what *you* can do, not someone else."

"Yeah, I know mom," I said. "I'm surprising myself with how well it's coming."

I couldn't believe Ted still was keeping his trap shut. But then I thought I heard a little chuckle.

"What Ted?" the old lady asked. "You wanted to say something?"

"No, it's nothing," he said. "I was just reminded of something."

"Ted, are you helping Daniel with this project?" the old man asked.

"Oh no, he has to do it on his own, pretty much. And Danny hasn't asked for my help, have you Danny?"

"Nah, it's coming along just fine," I said.

Later in our bedroom Ted said, "I can't believe you went to Professor Wheeling. How did you even know about him?"

I shrugged. "I went over to Princeton and asked for a science guy," I lied. I wasn't going to tell him I went through his stuff.

"A science guy?" Ted asked.

"You know, a professor type. They gave me his name. I looked him up and went to his place."

"You went to where he lives?"

"Yeah, it's a real dump, have you-"

"You went to his place!" Ted screamed. He was getting hot on me.

"Shh! I said. "Calm down."

"So you mentioned my name or what?"

"Nah, I told him mine, and he said he knew you, that's all. I got lucky."

"Are you crazy? The head of the physics department at Princeton University is going to help a kid with his science project?"

"Well, he is."

"Because you happened, by chance, to find out he's a Yankee fan, is that it? I wonder if Mrs.Sweet would have given you her husband's precious baseball stuff if she'd known you would give it away."

"I'm not giving it away." I did feel kind of shitty though, now that Ted put it that way.

"What did you say you'd give him?"

"Some cards, a uniform."

"A uniform? I would think that's worth a lot of money. Is it signed, too?"

"Yeah, Mize."

"This is so bad, you've outdone yourself. I can't even tell mom or dad about it. Giving away what you are, and making me a laughingstock in front of Wheeling and the guys."

"Those ham radio guys? Hey they're ok, but why do you like hanging around with guys like them?" I asked.

"What, instead of the delinquents who you call your friends?"

"At least we have fun. That ham radio stuff, I mean talking on a radio to people doesn't sound like too much of a gas to me."

"Look, just don't talk about this thing anymore. You're making your own rope. You'll hang yourself in the end, just like you always do."

I wasn't sure what he meant by that, at least in this case. But then, it seems I never do see it coming, the shit hitting the fan, I mean.

Next Saturday morning the phone rang.

"Daniel, it's for you," the old lady said. "It sounds like a man."

"Hello," I said.

"Hey, Danny, this is Sam, we've got your project ready."

"Really? Terrific," I said. The old lady was standing right over me practically. I couldn't have them pull right up to the house and deliver the damn thing, not with the chance she'd see the whole deal.

"Uh, ok, I'll be outside, you coming now?"

"Sure," Tweedledee said.

"Ok," I said and hung up.

"Who was that, Daniel?" my old lady asked.

"Oh, some guy. I'll see ya."

"Wait! Where are you going?"

"Over to Lance's. Gotta help him do something."

"You're up to something, aren't you, kiddo?"

"Up to something? No, that guy on the phone, he's some guy helping me and Lance with something. I'd better run."

"Daniel!" I heard her say behind me.

"Bye mom!" I yelled back and bolted out the door. I ran through some backyards to Lance's house, five houses down. His bedroom was upstairs, and I was hoping he was home. I picked up some pebbles and the third one that hit his window made him look out. I waved my arms and he opened it up.

"What?" he asked.

"Open your garage door, hurry!"

"What's up?"

"They're delivering my science fair project!"

"Who is?"

"I'll tell you all about it. Quick!"

He disappeared from the window. I heard him unlock the door from the inside, and I helped him open it.

"What are you up to now?"

"Just stay here. I'll be right back!"

I ran out to the street. A minute later, I saw the car and waved them down.

"What are you doing out in the street?" Tweedledee asked.

"Listen, I can't have you drop off this thing to my house. My parents will know you guys did it instead of me. If you pull in this driveway, we'll put it in my friend's garage."

"Yeah, ok," Tweedledum said. "But Wheeling wants his baseball stuff before we do that"

I'd forgotten all about it. Now I had to sneak that stuff out of the house.

"Ok, ok," I said. "Pull in here and I'll run home and get it."

They parked in front of the garage, which was in the back of the house. "Is that it?" I asked, seeing something in the backseat. It doesn't look like much."

"Yeah, don't worry," Tweedledee said. "It's not assembled, you have to do that on site. We need a table to show you how."

"We can put it in the basement," Lance said. "We've got a ping pong table."

"Good," Tweedledum said.

I ran back home and entered through the cellar door. I tiptoed up the stairs and opened the door a bit to peek into the kitchen, which was just off to the left. The old lady wasn't there, so I beat it through it and upstairs to my room. I had the collection in my closet, and fished out the cards and uniform. If I was seen I was dead. I couldn't chance it. I opened the front window, popped out the bottom of the screen, and slipped Mize's uniform into the bushes.

I almost hit the old man right in the head. He was moving away from where the uniform was, trimming. The noise he was making with the cutters kept him from hearing anything else. He had about ten feet to go until he got to the end of the hedge, and he would come back to pick the leaves up, sure as shootin'. I had to pick up the uniform before then.

I hightailed it down the stairs and out the basement. I saw the old lady gardening out back, so for the moment she was no problem. I went to the front, and made my way between the bushes and the house. I reached up and grabbed the uniform. The old man was just reaching the end of the house.

I ran across the front lawn, keeping close to the houses. I couldn't go out back because of the old lady. I was all out of breath when I made it back to Lance's.

"What the hell happened to you?" Tweedledee asked.

"He's up to no good, I can tell you that," Lance said. "These guys told me about the deal you made with that professor."

"Wow," I said.

"Yeah, we spent a hell of a lot of our time making this, so I hope this baseball stuff is worth it," Tweedledum said.

"Yeah, it is," I said.

"So kid, you got it?" Tweedledee said to Lance, pointing to the project.

"Piece a cake," Lance said.

"Ok, well, good luck," Tweedledum said.

"Ok, thanks," I said, and they were gone from my life, finally.

"This is a helluva thing they made, Danny," Lance said.

There was the earth, a shiny metal ball with a sign on it that said, 'EARTH'. It was connected to a metal base by a rod. Around the earth were eight small shiny balls, which were the satellites. Each of them was connected to the earth by two clear tubes at an angle. Inside each tube were lights. The lights lit up one at a time, so it looked like they were going up to each satellite and back down to earth. Each spot on earth that the lights came down to was a little box labeled, 'Transmission Base.' It was really cool. And that was the problem.

"It's unbelievable, Danny," Lance said.

"It's too good," I said. "No one will believe I did it."

A voice behind me said, "What's that thing?"

It was Lance's sister. She was sixteen, like Ted. She was a brain, too, but not too big in the looks department. And over the years she'd been nothing but a big pain in the ass to Lance and me whenever we were together.

"It's Danny's science fair project," Lance told her.

"What's with those balls, and that big metal thing in the middle?" she asked,

"They're not balls, they're satellites, and the big thing is the earth, see, it says it right there," I said snotly.

"What's a satellite?" she asked.

"It's too complicated-" I started to say, but she cut me off and said, "Oh, it's too complicated for me, but not for the likes of you, huh? Ha, Danny. Since when is Danny McTavish able to comprehend something and Julie Danvers not able?" She put her hands on her hips like she had a habit of doing. She was a real pain in the ass, like I said.

"Look, Julie," Lance said, "Our country is going to shoot off rockets and put these here satellites into an, what did you call it, Danny?"

"Orbit," I said.

"Yeah, orbit," he said, "and they go round and round the earth."

"They don't go round and round the earth," I told him. That's why they're stuck there like this."

"They'd fall right down you egghead," Julie said, looking at me.

"No, it doesn't work that way," I said. I didn't know what I was talking about, but I knew enough to know that they somehow wouldn't.

"What are these stupid lights for?" she asked. "And transmission stations?"

"Look-" I started to say, but she cut me off again.

"And where is your experiment, and hypothesis, and conclusion?" she asked.

"I'm workin' on it," I said.

"Oh, you forgot about it," she said.

"You failing science, Danny?" Lance asked me.

"Yeah, so far, but I made a deal with Jacobs that if I won the competition he'd promise to pass me."

"Why would he care?" Julie asked.

"Because he likes Ted. He said he didn't want to embarrass the family, plus he didn't want to have me again if I flunked."

"Did you do any of this, Danny?" Julie asked.

"Sure he did, didn't you Danny?" Lance asked.

I looked at Julie, and I could tell by the look on her face she knew I had as much to do with building the contraption in front of us as I would with the real satellites.

"I thought of it, though," I answered.

"You idiot, Jacobs will see right through it," she said.

Why was it bothering me that she was already the second person to tell me that?

The science fair was Tuesday night. That meant I had to write up the stuff about the project right away.

Ted could do it in his sleep, but there was no way he'd help me. The problem was there was no experiment; it just showed something. I looked at the magazine again showing the satellites around the earth. I had to make it simple. I got a sheet of that oak tag crap at the store and folded it nice so it stood up. The trouble with that was now I had three huge sections, and it would look funny if I didn't put something in each. I took a magic marker and wrote in the center: 'THE FUTURE OF COMMUNICATIONS and underneath it, 'By Danny McTavish.'. Underneath that I wrote: 'Satellites Orbit the Earth in Geosynchronous Orbit. This means they will remain stationary in orbit. Transmission Stations Will Beam Signals up to Satellites and Back Down Again to Next Transmission Station and So On.' On the left panel I put, 'Vanguard Program Creating Rockets to Send Satellites into Orbit.' On the right panel I put, 'Will Commies Win? The World Waits.'

I thought that last bit up after what Tweedledum and Tweedledee said, and I thought it would add some pizzazz.

Tuesday came, and when science class ended, Mr. Jacobs told me to stick around. When everyone left he said, "Well, did you finish your project?"

"It's all done," I told him.

"You think you can win?"

"I dunno. I think so. It's pretty cool."

"You'd better not embarrass yourself, McTavish."

"Oh no sir, I won't," I said.

"*Or* me, because how well my students do is a reflection on me," he said.

"Yes sir, I understand sir."

"Satellites, huh?"

"Yeah."

"Does Ted know about this?"

"Sort of," I said, "but he hasn't seen it."

"Be here by six-thirty to set up."

"Six-thirty," I nodded.

After dinner, me and the old lady and old man got in the car.

"Why is your project at Lance's?" the old man asked.

"It's kind of big, so it's on his ping pong table. But it's in pieces now so I have to put it all together. Lance and I put it in a box."

Lance's mom greeted us at the door.

"Well, hello there folks, come on in," she said. Then she said, " Henry, Barb, you must be so proud of Daniel."

"Well, I heard his project is quite something," the old man said.

"Oh yes, quite extraordinary," she agreed.

We made it into the basement and Lance's mom said, "I must confess, I saw it and have no idea what it's about."

"State of the art, as they say," the old man said, whatever that meant.

"Dad, I'll take this base, if you can get the box," I said.

"Yup," he said, eyeing the steel balls, "State of the art."

We got to school and carried the stuff into the gym where everybody was setting up. I found my spot, and set it up like Lance had shown me. I finished and hooked up the battery. The lights came on, one by one, up the tubes and down the tubes, one satellite and base station to another, all around the earth. I set the signboard up behind it.

"Danny, what is it?" the old man asked.

"Well, you can read all about it here," I answered. I left the old man and old lady alone, and worked my way around. There were about fifty projects. The closest to mine was on rocketry and looked complicated. The kid had built a miniature one about two feet high, and it was cut open in the middle so you could see the engine and crap. He had a picture of that guy Von Braun, and a history of rocketry, and some formulas even. I was surprised to see he had done some sort of experiment and hypothesis, but I didn't want to read about it so I left.

I thought mine had a shot to win. It was state of the art like my old man said. I think I knew what he meant, because most everyone's else was about old corny stuff, like about batteries and engines.

My folks drifted around and came to me, and the old lady said, "Daniel, there are a lot of wonderful projects, aren't there?"

"Uh huh," I agreed.

"Yours is the best though," she said. "It's marvelous. How did you do those lights? And it's so shiny. Henry dear, isn't it just so shiny?"

"Yes, very shiny Barb," the old man said.

"Daniel," he said.

"What, dad?"

"I'm very proud of you. You must have done a lot of research. I know you must have had help somewhere along the way, but I suppose that's ok."

"Yeah, the guys helped me some."

"Where did you come up with those steel balls?" he asked.

"Oh, we found them lying around," I said.

"Lying around?" he said. "I've never seen anything like it just lying around. And these lights, how do they work?"

"Oh, they're sequential," I remembered.

"Oh, I see," he said, I think confused as hell.

"Look," the old lady said. "The judges are gathering around your project, Danny." Don't you think you should be down there with it?"

"I dunno. They probably don't want me around, to hear their comments and stuff."

"I remember Ted was always winning," she said. "Let's hope they hang a blue ribbon on yours, too." She then actually hugged me. That wasn't too cool in front of all those science punk kids.

"They're staying there a long time," the old man said.

Finally the judges stopped looking at it and moved on.

"Let's go over and look," the old lady said.

As we got next to it, we passed Jacobs. He gave me one of those if looks could kill kind of deals. What the hell did I do wrong now?

Written on my display was 'DISQUALIFIED.' The old man said, "Disqualified?"

"Yes, what's the meaning of this, Daniel?" a voice behind us said. I recognized it as Jacob's.

"What?" I asked.

"Look," he said, and he pointed at my 'EARTH' sign on the big ball. One end of it had come off so it just hung there, and written into the metal underneath where it used to be was,

VAN DER GRAF GENERATOR
PROPERTY OF PRINCETON UNIVERSITY

"I, well," I stammered.

"Did you go to Princeton to do this?" the old lady asked.

"Well, sort of, " I admitted.

"You didn't steal these things, did you, Daniel?" she asked.

"Steal? No, of course not!"

"Who did this work?" Jacobs asked. He was hot.

"It was my idea, honest," I said.

"Who did the work, Danny?" the old man asked.

"Some guys, like I told you."

"What do you mean?" he asked. "You told us you got some help from your friends."

"Well, these are new friends. You can't disqualify me, I didn't do anything!" I said to Jacobs.

"That seems to be the problem," the old man said.

"No, I didn't mean it that way," I pleaded.

"Well Mr. Jacobs, this is not your problem," the old man said. "I'm sure we'll get to the bottom of this when we get home."

"No, there's no story!" I yelled. "I thought this whole thing up! I read about how Mr. Clarke said we'll put up these satellites and all," I said, pointing to the project.

"Come on, Daniel," my old lady said, but it was my turn to get hot. I'd given up two cards, including a DiMaggio, and a whole, signed uniform. There was no way I was going to be disqualified. And it wasn't my fault. It was those two goons, Tweedledum and Tweedledee. Hell, I'd report *them;* they're the ones who swiped that thing.

I ran behind the table, and ripped one of the satellite balls off the rod it was connected to. I chucked it, wires and all, towards Jacobs. I think it just missed his head.

"Daniel!" the old lady shouted, but I was really pissed off, so I barely heard her. I lifted earth from the base, ripped the battery wires from it, and ran back around, evading the old man who tried to grab me. Rods and wires and little satellite balls were hanging onto it, and I yelled to Jacobs, who was looking at me in shock, "Here it is, you fuckhead!" and I rolled it with both hands towards him. It didn't roll too far though what with all that crap hanging off of it.

"Daniel!" the old man hollered, and I managed to scream to the judges, "You can take your goddamn science fair and stick it up your ass!" He hauled me off to the car with the old lady bawling all over the place.

I'd been fucked again.

5

The shit hit the fan after that. They wanted to suspend me for the rest of the school year, which of course would mean I'd flunk everything. Jacobs was even considering filing charges against me, but he really couldn't since I was a kid. Then they talked about sending me to some sort of reform school.

I told the folks I was sorry about the whole thing; that I really just wanted to win, and pass science.

"It's because of Ted, isn't it?" the old lady asked. "Because you are trying to be like him."

"Well, sort of," I said.

And then she said to the old man, "Oh Henry, it's our fault". And she went on about how they love me just as much as Ted and how I did what I did to please them and all that rot, which was sort of true when it came right down to it. I didn't tell them about the deal I had made with Wheeling with the baseball stuff.

The folks and I had a meeting with the school principal, and she told them I'd be suspended for a week. I'd told them all how I'd do nothing but study my ass off, how I didn't want to be left behind.

So I stayed home the whole week, getting the homework assignments from Jerry or Lance on the phone.

"You're famous around here, you know," Jerry told me.

"Really?" I said. "What's everybody saying?"

"Well, some of the kids saw what you did, you know, the square kids. Oh yeah, they're real anxious to tell everybody what happened. A couple kids said the satellite you threw hit Jacobs in the head. Another said it hit his neck."

"Nah, I didn't hit him at all," I said. "I just threw it at him to make a point. I could have hit him if I'd really wanted to." I think I meant to hit him, actually, but I wasn't sure. "What else did they say?"

"That you told them to stick it up their ass! That really true?"

"Yeah, I think so."

"That's the goddamn funniest thing ever, you know that Danny."

"Yeah, but my folks and all them don't think so."

"You going away to reform school?" Lance asked.

"Nah, I don't think so. I told them I'd study and not fail, you know, the usual crap."

"Well, you better man, or you *will* fail."

"I don't think it makes any difference what I do, Jacobs is sure to flunk me."

"The chicks really dig what you did," Jerry said.

"Yeah, sure, I'll bet Tina really is pissed we broke up."

"Forget Tina, man. You'll have your pick when you come back."

"Uh huh," I said. "I'll bet they're all dying to get their hands on a maniac."

"You know how the chicks are. They like notoriety, you know, guys like Capone."

"Where the hell you come up with that idea?" I said.

"I don't know, it's just true. I mean, them guys had the chicks hangin' off them all the time, right?"

"You idiot, that's because those guys had the money. Plus they'd knock them dames off if they didn't keep hanging all over them."

"Well, you'll see. I just wish I had seen it," Jerry said.

"Yeah, it was a regular riot."

"How come they disqualified you, anyway? Nobody seems to know."

"You remember that the big ball had the earth sign on it?"

"Yeah, I think so."

"Well, it sort of fell off. The two nitwits from Princeton who put it together didn't stick it on so good, and they're was some crap written underneath it, right on the ball."

"What?" Jerry asked.

"That it belonged to Princeton. So then the whole story came out; they even accused me of stealing the damn thing."

"I wonder if those Princeton guys got in trouble."

"Nah, I'm sure nobody gives a shit. The professor is happy. He got his baseball stuff."

"Yeah, you gave that stuff away for nothing, it turns out, Danny."

"No shit," I agreed.

"Hey, you think you could get that stuff back?" Jerry asked.

"Back? What do you mean?"

"What do you mean, what do I mean? I think you got robbed. He didn't do it himself. He turned it over to them creeps who screwed up."

I was beginning to see the logic of it. "Yeah, keep talking," I said.

"Well, that's it. It's his fault it wasn't done right. Look, what we do is kind of the responsibility of our teachers, right?"

I remembered what Jacobs had told me, about how what we students did was a reflection on him.

Good old Jerry was right. That professor was a son of a bitch, for sure. The thought of my precious baseball stuff on display in that rotten joint of his made me sick.

"So what do you think?" he said.

"I think we need to plan an operation," I said.

"We?" he asked.

"You don't think I can pull this heist off myself, do you?"

"I don't need to get in hot water like you already are, man," Jerry said. "Besides, you can't afford to get in any more trouble. You do, they're sure to send you away, maybe for good."

"Gee thanks, then why the hell did you tell me I should take it back?" I said. "That's why you have to do it."

"No way, it's robbery."

"What the hell you talking about?" I said. "Like you said, the stuff's really still mine. And you'll have notoriety, and get the chicks, remember?"

"I can't do it," he said. "If I do it, it's robbery, if you do it you're just taking back what you think is still yours. Hey wait! What if you talked to that professor guy, and tell

him what happened. Maybe he'd just give you your stuff
back!"

"I'd like to think that but there's no way he'd give it
back. He's an asshole."

"How do you know?" You don't even know the
guy!" Jerry said.

"You should see his crummy place, with the books
all over the place," I said.

"He married?" Jerry asked.

"Nah, I don't see how. Not with all that crap all over
the place."

"Good, that makes it easier."

"Yeah, well, I can't think about doing anything now,
seeing as I'm grounded for the rest of the week."

"You have to do it now," Jerry said. "That professor
guy will be in class during the week. He'll be home on the
weekend."

"I can't do it alone. And you're in class."

"So what are you going to do?"

"I don't know, I'll come up with something. Thanks
for the idea, you shit."

"Yeah sure," he said. "No problem."

So now, because of that numbskull Jerry, sticking in
my craw was the thought of my stuff in the professor's
place, and I can't stand it.

It was Tuesday, and I remembered the old lady
played cards with the ladies on Wednesday. The bowling
alley opened at ten, so the old man would be gone too.
Maybe I could pull off the heist tomorrow.

"So Danny, how is the studying coming?" the old
lady asked that night at dinner.

"Swell, mom. I'm hitting the books hard."

"You'd better, son," the old man said.

I looked over at Ted, who was smirking into his plate. Oh, how he'd loved it when he heard the story about what happened that night. I told him how those idiot friends of his had screwed up, and all he did was laugh. He thought it was the goddamn funniest thing he'd ever heard.

"Yeah, well, you can tell your buddies they fucked me big time," I'd told him.

"You guys probably knocked it off," he'd said.

"What do you mean?" I asked. "It was on there when I set it up."

"But you must've loosened it, so it was ready to go," he said.

"Oh, so now it's my fault that friggin' thing fell off. You can't even admit your friends screwed up. Just because they're ham radio physics creeps, and I'm dumb little Danny McTavish." I hated him, just then. They were all the same, those high-assed scholarly types. Assholes to the end. I wondered if Einstein was that way, but I didn't think so. I think he was different, somehow.

"Well, do you think that contraption came with a guarantee?" Ted said. "It's amazing the thing worked at all, after you guys got a hold of it. But maybe it was justice, the way it turned out. You know if you'd won, you wouldn't have deserved it."

"If I'd lost, I'd lost. Nobody said I had to get screwed like I did."

"Like I told you, you always give yourself enough rope to hang yourself."

He was hopeless.

Anyway, at dinner, the old lady said, "Now Danny, I have bridge tomorrow at eleven. I don't want you going anywhere. Can I trust you?"

"Ma, I've got to keep hitting the books. You think I want to be left behind?"

"That's not what I asked."

"Sure, I'm staying right here, tomorrow," I said. Well, I did up until just after eleven, that is. I hitched back over to Princeton, and went to the science building. I asked some broad if the professor was around. She said he'd be in class all day. Which is just what I wanted to hear.

I knew I had to be home by two to be safe. My Timex said twelve fifteen. I walked over to the professor's place. I tried the front door just for kicks, but it was locked.

"Can I help you?" someone asked.

I froze, and then turned around. An old bag was standing in front of me. The last thing I needed was for the professor to hear that some kid had been snooping around his joint.

"Oh, hi," I said. "I was just wondering if the professor was home."

"No, I'm sorry," she said. "He has classes all day. Is there something I can help you with?"

"No thanks, that's ok."

"Are you a friend of the professor's?" she asked.

"Well, our families are, yeah. The professor borrowed something from me, actually, that I need for school. That's why I'm not there, you see," I said.

"I'm his landlord," she said. "If you really must have it back, I could let you in. But tell me, what is it, young man?"

"Some baseball stuff, a uniform and some cards."

"Oh, I see. Yes, I know the professor's a big baseball fan. I know that much. He brought me a ball from a game, once. What's your name?"

"You don't say?" I had to think of a name that made sense, and fast. "It's, uh Barry. I have a brother, Sam."

"But they're graduate students of his, aren't they? I've met them. The uh, I'm trying to think of their last name."

"Oh, no, I mean to say they're my brothers. Older brothers. It's all in the family, ha."

"Oh, I see, why didn't you say so before? They're such nice young men."

She fished some keys from a little purse and found the one she wanted, and opened the front door. Man, I couldn't believe she bought the story.

I looked everywhere, and couldn't find any of it. I couldn't look in the guy's closet, seeing as the old bag was standing right over me the whole time.

"Doesn't seem to be here," I said.

"Perhaps they're at his office," she said.

Shit, why didn't I think of that first? Damn. "Maybe you're right!" I said.

"Maybe he's displaying them over there, you never know," she said.

"Well, thanks for everything."

"Of course, glad I could be of help."

"Say, do you think you could do me a big favor?" I asked.

"Yes, young man?"

"Do you think you could maybe not mention anything about this to the professor, about me stopping by, I mean. I feel a little funny about it, if you know what I mean."

"Well, certainly he'd like-"

"In fact, I'll just mention it to him when I see him, you know, over at his office!"

"Well, yes, I suppose so, you will won't you," she said, and smiled.

"Well, ok then, goodbye."

"Bye, bye," she said.

I was breathing a whole lot easier when I left. I had to hope the old bag would come through and keep her trap shut. My Timex said one o'clock. I wanted to pay Tweedledum and Tweedledee a visit to give them a piece of my mind, but I wasn't sure I had time, and besides, it was too risky. If I located the goods and swiped it, they'd find out and tell Wheeling they knew it was me who took it.

I snooped around the science building and lo and behold I heard a familiar voice coming from a nearby room.

"-and so the electron loses energy, returning to the d orbit, thereby the molecule emits a photon of light blah blah blah-". I had to find his office fast. It wasn't on the near side of the hall. I figured it had to be down the hall, past the room he was lecturing in. And the goddamn door was open!

How I could get past it without being seen was the big question. There was only one way. I took off my shoes and ran as fast as I could past the door. I slowed down a few feet past. Wheeling didn't miss a beat; he just went right on talking.

Four doors down, I saw a sign on the wall next to it,

Professor Lawrence Wheeling
Physics

I saw it as soon as I looked in his office. Mize's uniform was on the wall, inside a picture frame covered with glass. The nerve of that guy showing off what was still really mine. I wanted to take his stinking pipe and shove it down his stinking throat. I looked around for the cards for a few seconds, but couldn't find them. I gave that search up quick. I reached up and took the uniform off the wall, and put it on his desk. I took off the back, and the uniform came out with it. It was stuck to the back by some pins, so I pulled them out. I realized I should have brought a bag, but since I didn't, I rolled up the uniform nice and tight, and then snuck out into the hallway with it under my arm.

I hightailed it back past the room where Wheeling was still blabbing away, picked up my shoes, and never looked back.

I made it home just before two o'clock, ran upstairs, chucked the uniform in the box in my closet and jumped on my bed.

I was all out of breath I think as much from excitement as from running. I'd done it. I pulled off the heist, without a hitch.

Then I started to think about it. I was cooked, and I knew it. Wheeling would know it was me who took the uniform. And probably his old bag of a landlord would squeal on me.

I heard the old lady come home. Man, I was still breathing hard. I had to calm down fast.

"Danny, are you there?" she called up.

"Yeah, sure mom. I'm just studying, you know."

Good to hear it, dear."

I began to imagine the look on the old professor's face when he saw the uniform was gone. I'd give anything to see it.

I gloated about it all day and the next. And then late afternoon on Thursday, I heard the doorbell ring. I got a funny feeling in my stomach when I heard it.

The old man was greeting someone, and then I heard footsteps into the living room. I could hear talking, but couldn't make out the words. A couple of minutes went by, and then the old man called up to me, "Daniel, come down here, please." I didn't like the please word; it always meant trouble.

The trip down the stairs was the longest of my life. I could see the legs and shoes of someone sitting in a chair. I knew they had to be Wheeling's. Then I saw across from his the shoes of my folks. My legs started to shake real bad.

I reached the bottom of the stairs, and my and the professor's eyes met.

"Yeah dad?" I somehow squeaked out.

The old man said something I couldn't believe. He said, "Barb, would you leave us dear?"

"What?" she asked.

"Please dear," and he put his hand on hers. She got up and went past me and gave me the look over with a sad pair of eyes. I figured the old man didn't want her to see the sight of blood. I wondered if I would ever see her again.

"Daniel," the old man said, "I think you know Professor Wheeling here."

"Yes sir," I said.

"The professor has told your mother and I the story of how you came to him for help with the science fair project. And how you offered some of your baseball collection to him in exchange for that help."

"Yes sir." I felt like total crap, there's no two ways about it. I figured I might as well start packing right then and there, since I'd be shipped off to reform school right quick. I'd really done it this time, and broken the last straw, as they say.

"The professor says the uniform you gave him has been stolen. I take it you now have it in your possession?"

"Yes sir."

And then he said, "Professor, did you hear what happened to that science fair project?"

"Can't say I did, no," he said.

"Well, your graduate students, whom you entrusted to do it in your stead, did a less than perfect job." He told him about how the sign came off, and underneath it revealed that the ball had been the property of Princeton, which led to me being disqualified.

"Really?" Wheeling said. "I'm sorry it happened, but I don't see what this has to do with-" he started to say, but the old man waved him off.

"Seeing as your graduate students were acting under your instructions to help my son, do you not feel responsible for their actions? Namely, that they stole property belonging to the University?"

"Well, I-" Wheeling again started to say, and then the old man stood up.

"Professor Wheeling, I think it in the best interest of all of us, that we drop this entire matter altogether. Keep the cards Daniel gave you. I think under the circumstance that is more than fair."

Wheeling took a deep breath, and nodded his head. He got up and walked past me, without looking at me. The old man led him to the front door and Wheeling left.

The old man closed the door. I didn't know what to think anymore. What the hell was he going to do to me? He walked over and put his hand on my shoulder.

"Danny," he said. "Let's forget about the whole thing. Just promise your mother and I one thing."

"What's that dad?" I asked,

"That you pass this semester. Let's take one thing at a time."

"Yes sir," I said, and went upstairs and bawled my brains out. Ted was studying at his desk, and never said a word.

6

I ended up passing all my courses, even science. I managed to get a C on the final exam, and Jacobs gave me a final grade of D. I think he just wanted to be done with me. And who could blame him? I was getting tired of myself, quite frankly.

It wasn't always this way. Once upon a time, I was a sweet, innocent kid. Nobody was after me. Nobody hated me. Nobody had any reason to think Danny McTavish was a shit. There were no Kowalskis and Tina's old man, or Jacobs Tweedledee and Tweedledum. There was no one who wanted to get their grubby hands around my throat. And no one who's throat I wanted to get my hands around. Once upon a time Ted was my big brother who could do no wrong; a guy I had fun hanging around with.

I needed to get away. As it turned out, we always hit the road right after school let out to head up to my uncle's place in upstate New York. This yeahr there was a bonus. Ted couldn't come. He said he had a special project to work on, so the folks let him stay behind. That suited me just fine. I could be away from him for a whole week.

When I heard he wasn't coming, I celebrated by pretending to be disappointed. "Ted, c'mon, won't you come along?" I asked. "We'll have fun up at the lake like we used to. What do you say, huh?"

"Yeah, sure Danny," he said. "I'm sure you're real disappointed. But I've got a project to work on." He said he was working on his future, something I'd probably never think about.

I got a good chuckle out of that one. I imagined him and his square buddies having a grand old time working out equations or some such. Maybe he'd introduce his high school buddies to Tweedledum and Tweedledee, and they'd have a party. Like I said before, I wished Ted good luck with his future of passing a chalk across a board, dreaming up all kinds of theories and crap. I wanted my life to stick to realities, like having fun and being with good-looking chicks. Yeah, I knew I'd have to eventually make a living, but just not his way. I had plenty of time to figure something out.

It was a five-hour drive to the lake. My folks figured we'd better leave no later than three so we wouldn't get there past dark.

We said goodbye to dear old Ted. The old lady gave him hugs and kisses, and the old man shook his hand. It was the first time we'd be splitting up as a family.

"Well, see ya," I said.

"Yeah, sure," he replied. "Don't let the bed bugs bite." It was the first time I'd heard him say that since we were little kids, when we went camping a few times with the old man.

"Yeah, you too," I said.

And then he broke into this big grin. The whole time he waved us down the driveway, he had the same face. Was he that happy to be rid of me? Man, I didn't know I was that much of a pain in the ass to him.

We hit the road, stopping a few times for gas and once to get a bite to eat. After a few hours, the road started to climb into the mountains, and the air got a little cooler. I watched the evergreens as we passed them by. The air seemed to be cleaner, too. Yeah, it would be good to get away. This trip always made me realize how crowded it was where we lived. Maybe when I was off on my own, I'd move to the country. There wouldn't be any hot, smelly bowling alleys. No guys like Kowalski and them types. Just me and the countryside. I'd get married to the most beautiful broad in the world. See, I was planning for my future, just like Ted.

I stuck my head out the window, feeling the wind in my face and hair. One of my old lady's favorite songs was playing on the radio, and she sang along with good old Perry Como,

> *"Find a wheel and it goes round, round, round,*
> *As it skims along with a happy sound,*
> *As it goes along the ground, ground, ground,*
> *'Til it leads to the one you love..."*

She looked over at the old man, looking especially happy as she did whenever we headed up this way.

> *"In the night you see the oval moon,*
> *going round and round in tune..."*

I owed the old lady a week of good behavior. I vowed right then and there that I wouldn't mess up. I was suddenly feeling pretty good about myself. I had passed my courses, working my ass off to do it. I'd gotten my uniform back from that bastard professor. My slate seemed to clean as the miles clicked by. Even the folks seemed happy with me.

We pulled into uncle Ray's driveway around eight, the gravel popping under the tires. He and aunt Betty and their two snotty kids came out to greet us.

"Where is Ted?" they all wondered. The old lady told them the story, and how sorry he was he couldn't make it. And then my cousin Ray Jr. piped up,

"Hey, Danny, ya think I can sleep in the bunk beds with you? You can have the top bunk if you want. Huh mom, can I, huh?"

Christ almighty, we'd been at the joint not two minutes and the punk already was making me wish I could turn around and go home.

"We'll see, Ray," his old lady told him. We'll see, my ass. Just go ahead and ask me if it's ok, ok?

"Tell them about the bonfire, mom," my cousin Beth said. I think she was eight, which I guess made her two years younger than Ray Jr.

"After supper, we'll all head over to a bonfire. A bunch of families planned a get together," aunt Betty told us.

"That sounds like fun," my old lady said.

We ate with my folks and Ray and Betty shooting the shit about the good and the bad during the yeahr. We only really saw them twice a yeahr, at this time and Christmas, so they had some catching up to do.

I tried to avoid Ray Jr., but he kept asking me if he could sleep in the bunkroom, and his old lady kept telling him to cool it. I wanted to reach over and push his face into his plateful of mashed potatoes.

Dark was coming on, and the lake was turning black. Lights from homes across the lake danced in the water. The peepers were out, making a racket.

"We ladies will clean up and then we'll all head out to the bonfire," aunt Betty said.

We men headed out to the deck overlooking the lake. We sat on those wooden chairs that were about as comfortable as rocks. The guys who designed them must have learned furniture design at a torture chamber or something.

Uncle Ray was my mom's brother, so my old man and he didn't talk much at all during the yeahr. Ray asked him how the bowling alley business was.

"Steady. The usual," he said.

"What about them new automatic pin setters?" Ray asked.

"What about them?" the old man asked, but he knew what Ray was getting at.

"Well, Henry, maybe it's time to bite the bullet, invest in putting them in your place, or better yet, open up a new bigger place, why don't you? Them new places, I hear they got one with sixty-six lanes."

"That's big bucks, Ray. I haven't found a tree yet that grows it."

"Other people are finding the dough somehow, Henry. It's the future. You've got to go with it, or move out of the way."

The old man didn't say anything to that, but I knew he was worried about what Ray was bringing up. The fact of the matter was, pin boys were going to be a thing of the past, and everyone knew it.

I thought about what Ted had said about how we were rocketing from the Atomic Age to the Space Age. And then I thought of what the old man had said about my science fair project, and the words just came tumbling out,

"State of the art," I said.

"What's that Danny?" the old man asked.

"It's like you said, dad. State of the art. That new automatic pin setting gadgetry is state of the art, isn't it?"

His chair creaked he was rocking it so hard. "Yeah, son, state of the art. I guess you could say it is."

"What's that?" uncle Ray asked.

"Tell him Danny," the old man said.

"About what dad?" I asked.

"About your science fair project."

"Oh. Well, we're building rockets right now that will send these things into orbit around the earth. They'll just stay up there, about a hundred miles up."

"What are you talkin' about son?" Ray asked.

"They're called satellites. They'll be left up there-"

"Won't they just fall down, Danny?" Ray Jr. asked.

"You would think they would," I said, "but they won't, not if they're high enough anyway. If we put enough of them up there, we'll be able to bounce signals off them like television programs. That way we'll be able to watch stuff happening from all over the world."

"Sounds like a bunch of hogwash to me, Henry," uncle Ray said.

"No really, it's-" I started to say, but I stopped cold. I suddenly realized I was sounding just like Ted had that night at the dinner table. And the scary thing was, I kind of felt good about it. It felt ok making a numbskull out of uncle Ray like the numbskull he was.

"What's the matter, Danny?" the old man asked.

I looked up at the sky. Man, the stars were bright and close looking. "Nothing," I said.

"You know, Henry," uncle Ray said. "If something happens to the bowling alley, well, you could come up here. There's always a place at the hardware store for you."

The old man didn't say anything, so I said it for him,

"Thanks, uncle Ray, but I think my dad will always have the bowling alley. Won't you dad?" I'd be damned if my old man would work in someone else's hardware store.

"Oh, sure, son," he said. "But some day I'll get rid of it. It's nothing for you boys. It's a living, is all it is. You and Ted will be living in a different kind of world. A world of rockets, and satellites, and flying automobiles."

"And automatic pin setters," Ray said, the shit.

Just then, the ladies came out to join us.

"Time to go boys," aunt Betty said.

We walked along the edge of the lake in single file by Aunt Betty's flashlight. After a few minutes, we could see light flickering in the tree tops up ahead. We came to a clearing. In the center was the fire, and around it were a bunch of logs with people sitting on them.

When we came into the light, Aunt Betty introduced us to the group, and the seven of us clumped together on a couple of logs. Some of the people looked familiar.

A guy told a dumb story which was supposed to be funny, but wasn't. The grownups chuckled anyway, like they always do no matter how unfunny the story is. I started to get real sleepy, and I could barely keep my eyes open.

I guess I saw things differently all of a sudden, because for the first time I noticed a girl across the fire, and she was staring at me. She gave a little wave when our eyes met. I wondered how long she had been eyeing me, and how I had missed seeing her until that moment. She looked to be about my age. She was sitting between two broads, one I guessed to be her old lady. The glow from the fire lit her face, and a pretty one it was. She'd take her eyes away from me, and look at the fire. Then she'd look up, and I'd look away. We kept doing that sort of thing for a while. There was nothing else we could do. I was stuck between my old lady and old man. Time crept along, and every time I looked her over she got better looking. But my eyes kept getting heavier and heavier.

"*Danny, don't nod off like that! Wake up!*

"*What dad?*"

"*Wake up, son, it's rude to fall asleep. That girl across the fire wants your attention. She likes you, Danny, how can you fall asleep on her?*"

"*Huh?*"

"*That lovely girl over there,*" *dad said, pointing.*

I put his hand down. "*Dad, don't point like that! It's embarrassing. I don't want her to know you've noticed her too.*"

"*Go get her boy!*"

"*Gee, I dunno dad.*"

"*I've never told you this, son, but you're the great hope for this family.*"

"*I am? How?*"

"*Well, Ted, he's brilliant, but let him be concerned with that stuff, you know, outer space and all that. I need you to give your mother and I beautiful grandchildren.*"

"*How do you mean?*"

"Well Ted, he'll never score big in the lady department. We both know that."

"Uh huh."

"So your mother and I are leaving it up to you, like I said. So go see that lovely girl over there." he pointed again. *"It's ok that I point, son. She's expecting you."*

"You sure, dad?"

"Go get her!"

I stood up and walked around the outside of the circle of people. I made it over to where the girl was sitting, and stood behind her. She turned around and raised her left arm so I could take her hand. She smiled.

"I thought you'd never come, Danny."

I took her hand, and she stood. For some reason, the people around her paid no attention.

We walked away. "How do you know my name?"

"Oh Danny, don't you remember me?"

"No," I was embarrassed to admit.

"I'm that little girl who was always admiring you so, all these years we've been coming to the lake. But you never noticed me."

"So what's your name?" hoping when she told me it would sound familiar.

"Guess."

"I can't."

"Please."

"I really haven't any idea."

Doesn't the name Jessica mean anything to you?"

As much as I wanted to nod my head yes, I couldn't. "No, can't say it does."

"I'm teasing you Danny. I really didn't expect you to know. After all, I've always been too afraid to say anything to you."

"Why didn't you?"

"You wouldn't have paid any attention to me, even if I had. I wore glasses and braces until this summer. But now that they're off, haven't I blossomed into a real beauty?"

"My goodness, you have, yes." I said, meaning it entirely.

"That was nice of your dad to wake you up. You'd fallen asleep, you know."

"Sorry, but you did notice me noticing you, right?"

"Oh yes! Come."

She led me by the hand along a path through woods. We came to a cabin on the lake.

"Let's sit on the swing," she said.

She ran up the porch steps pulling me along. We sat on a double swinger.

"Tell me sweet things, Danny."

I looked out into the darkness. Stars twinkled between the moving branches. "Look," I said, pointing up. "Soon, things are going to change forever."

"How do you mean, Danny?"

"When we look up in the night sky, we'll see points of light moving."

"Moving lights in the sky?"

"Satellites!"

Jessica stood up, angry. "Danny! How can you say something like that? You sound just like your silly brother, Ted!"

"How do you know my brother Ted?"

"Hasn't he been here with you every yeahr?"

"Oh yeah."

"Well, he's always bored me with his talk. I was so happy he didn't come this yeahr. I thought you were different. I thought you were exciting, mischievous, and I could have you all to myself! I'm finished with you!"

"I am different! You don't know me! Give me another chance, please!"

She sat back down, and looked into my eyes and held my hand. "Go ahead Danny, tell me something sweet."

"Would you like to see my dad's bowling alley someday?"

"What?"

"You could watch me set 'em up-"

She stood up again, angry. "What! You know your days of being a pin boy are numbered, Danny. Ha! And what would you have me be, a waitress in a stupid bowling alley just like your pretty little mother?"

"No! It's not what I meant, honest!"

"I'm done with you Danny, for real this time. You blew your chance."

"No, listen please," and I began to sing,

"In the night you see the oval moon,

going round and round in tune."

But she didn't hear; she was gone. I sat there on the swing, feeling lonelier than I'd ever felt. I'd been abandoned by the one I was supposed to love. I'd let my parents down.

"Jessica? Please come back!" I wanted to get up, but my legs wouldn't work. "Please, Jessica, just one more chance!" Somehow, I finally was able to make my legs move, but only very slowly. I got out of the swing, and walked like I *was stuck in thick mud. I made my way to the lake side of the cabin.   "Jessica?" I called, but there was no answer.   I walked down a path towards the water, which was white with moonlight. I saw a dark shape in front of it. As I got closer, I could tell the shape was two people holding each other. They were kissing.*

"Hey who is that? Jessica?" They stopped kissing, and the boy looked at me.

"You blew it, Danny," he said, and gave me a wink.

"Jerry? What are you doing here?"

"I came to do what I knew you couldn't. And all I had to do was follow your advice about the chicks. You know, advertise yourself and say what's on your mind. That's all you had to do, Danny."

"I thought I did that, didn't I Jessica?"

"Nah," Jerry said. "You started talking about that satellite crap. Who wants to hear that?"

"Not me!" Jessica said, and they both laughed.

"You're such a disappointment, Danny," a voice behind me said.

I turned to see my mother standing on the path.

"But mom. I, I just can't win! When I act like myself, I get in trouble. When I say things like Ted would say, it's no good either."

"Your father asked you to do just one thing right, and you couldn't do it. Look at this lovely girl, who's loved you so long. The both of you would have brought us such lovely grandchildren."

"It's not too late, mom."

I turned to Jessica. "Hey, Jessica, baby, let me show you how a real man kisses. It's like this see..." but she paid

*no attention to me, and she and Jerry just kept going at it
like there was no tomorrow...*

I woke up in a cold sweat. The dream I'd had was
coming back to me. The girl I'd seen at the bonfire was out
there somewhere. She had become the mystery girl who I
had to meet. I wasn't going to talk to her about satellites
when I did, that was for sure.

I got out of bed and made my way to the kitchen.
Everyone was in the breakfast room eating.

"Good morning, sleepyhead!" Ray Jr. said.

"You passed out, Daniel," my old lady said.

"Yeah," I said." I don't remember even the walk
back to the cabin."

"That's because I carried you, son," my old man
said.

"You carried me?" Oh great. I imagined my mystery
girl watching big old me with my sleepy head on my
mother's shoulder, and then her watching as the old man
lifted me up and carried me away. I'd picked a hell of a time
to sleep like I was dead.

I planned on asking Aunt Betty if she might know
the I.D. of a certain chick who had been at the fire, but of
course I couldn't ask her in front of anyone else.

"Hey Danny, we gonna hit the skis this morning?"
Ray Jr. asked.

I sat down at the breakfast table. I looked out at the
lake. It was a crummy looking day.

"Are you not feeling well Daniel?" the old lady
asked.

I stretched and yawned. "Nah, I'm ok, really," I said.
"I guess I just slept hard." I think the dream I'd had did me

in. Maybe I'd been stuck under the covers trying to move my legs, and that's why they felt like I was dragging them through thick mud.

"Ray, did you sleep in the top bunk?" I asked.

"Sure did. You didn't even know, did ya?"

"Nope."

"I think I heard you talking in your sleep," he said.

"Really? What did I say?" Oh god, why did I ask that?

You kept yelling, "No, No! Don't leave me behind! or something."

Beth giggled. "Who was doing that, Danny?"

"Beats me," I shrugged and tried to laugh.

"Some girl, I'll bet," Uncle Ray said.

"I don't think so," the old lady said. "I think Daniel's had his full of the opposite sex, at least for a while, haven't you Danny?"

What the hell was she talking about? Did she know about Tina? Or Tina's old man? Or Tina's old lady? What did my old lady know about any of that crap?

"Uh, yeah, mom," I said.

"What did he do now?" Beth asked.

Could I ever get any peace?

"Just a little problem, is all," the old lady said.

"He get a girl pregnant or somethin' aunt Barb?" Ray Jr. asked.

I put my hands over my ears and shook my head.

"Ray!" I heard aunt Betty yell.

"No, nothing like that. A girl was very unfair to your cousin," the old lady said.

She was? Yeah, she was. How did she know about that?

"Daniel and this girl were getting along just fine, and she started spreading these awful rumors about our poor Daniel," the old lady said.

She knew about my hitting on Tina's old lady! I think.

"Anyway, they don't bear repeating," she added.

Why was she bringing up this crap, and in front of these people? What the hell was she thinking?

"Danny got in trouble, Danny got in trouble," Beth was saying.

"Beth!" aunt Betty said.

"So we water skiing or what, Danny?" Ray Jr. asked again.

"Yeah, sure," I said. Anything to get out of the house.

"Drive carefully if you do, Daniel," my old lady said.

"Yeah, no sweat, mom. I've been driving these guys around for a long time now."

"Well, your brother's not here," she said.

"He-"

"Is that all right with you and Ray, Betty?" the old lady asked.

"He's a good driver, aren't you Danny?" Ray Jr. asked.

"Since your brother's not here, I should go too," my old man said. "That way you can ski."

"No, that's ok," I said.

After I ate and dressed, the two snots and I made it down to the dock. Uncle Ray had an eighteen footer. It was still pretty shitty out, but I liked being on the water with it. I liked to go fast. Open it up a bit. Of course, I wouldn't be able to while I was pulling the little shits.

She started right up and we headed out. I cruised along at about twenty-five knots. There was kind of a protected area, a bay like across the lake where everyone liked to ski, so I aimed for it. When we got there, no one else was around. I pulled the boat up to near the shoreline, and Ray hopped into the water with the skis. I eased the boat forward, and when the line got taught, I throttled up, and Ray popped up. He was pretty good for a little punk, I had to hand him that much.

"Watch this!" he yelled. Damned if he didn't come close to doing a three-sixty before he lost it. He tried a few more times, but he couldn't make it all the way around.

"My turn," Beth said.

When Ray got in the boat, he asked Beth, "You gonna try it?"

"Sure, I can do it," she said.

So she tried a few times, and the last time she nearly did it.

"Again, Danny," she said.

"Ok," I said. "Let's see you make it this time."

I eased forward to tighten the line and not too far in front of us, cutting across our front in the main part of the lake, was another boat. Two girls were in it. The one sitting next to the driver closer to me looked over and waved.

My mystery girl.

I gunned it.

"Hey!" I heard behind me. I'd forgotten all about the little creep in the water. I turned around and she was floating behind the rope. I'd probably come close to ripping her fucking arms off.

"Hey Danny, what you doin' anyways?" Ray Jr. asked.

I pulled the boat around to where Beth was in the water. "I think you've had enough," I said.

"No way, Danny," Beth said. "You said I'd get another chance!"

"Yeah, well, I think we should head home."

"No!" she yelled.

"We just started, Danny," Ray Jr. said.

"Hey Ray, you see those girls that just went by?" I asked.

"Yeah, what about 'em? Oh, so that's what this is about. Your mom said to stay away from girls, Danny."

"Who were they, do you know?"

"Yeah, but I'm not tellin'," he said.

"Listen-"

"We ski as long as we want, then I'll tell you who they are," Ray Jr. said.

"You don't know, you're just saying that," I said.

"Oh yeah?" he said.

"The one who waved. What's her name?"

"I'll tell you when we get back."

"C'mon Danny!" Beth yelled.

"Tell me now, Ray, or I'll go after them!"

"Ok, ok," he said. "It's Jane Melrose."

"You better not be lyin'" I said.

"I ain't lyin', Danny," Ray Jr. said. "Why would I lie? When we get back, you can ask about her. You'll see. My mom knows where she lives. Then you can kiss her all you want."

"Shut up," I said.

The kids skied around for a while longer. I didn't spy the girls the rest of the time we were out.

"Did you all have fun?" Aunt Betty asked when we got back to the cabin.

"We sure did, didn't we Danny?" Ray Jr. said, with a stupid grin on his face.

"I almost did a complete circle on skis, mommy," Beth said.

"How wonderful," aunt Betty said.

It wasn't until later in the afternoon that I had my chance. We were all outside on the deck, and aunt Betty said she'd go get some crap for us to snack on.

"I'll help," I piped up.

We were in the kitchen, when I slipped her the question, "Hey, aunt Betty. You ever hear of a girl by the name of Jane Melrose?"

"Oh yes, nice girl,"

"Well, I saw her today and last night. I kind of thought maybe, you know I could-"

"Actually, that would be wonderful if you asked her to the dance. Is that what you're thinking?"

"Dance? I didn't know-"

"At the municipal building by the lake. It's Friday night. Anyone can come. They'll be lots of young people like you. But it would be wonderful if you asked Jane to it. She's so shy, I don't think she'd come, otherwise."

"Really?"

"Would you like her number?"

"Sure," I said.

She gave it to me, and I went into the den to dial her up. A guy answered,

"Hello?"

"Hi, is Jane there?"

"Yes, Who's this?"

"My name's Danny McTavish. I come up to the lake and stay with my uncle Ray and aunt Betty. The Reynolds.

"Oh sure, hold on," he said.

A minute late, I heard a girl's voice,

"Hello?"

"Oh, hi," I said. "This Jane?"

"Uh huh."

"This is Danny McTavish. I-"

"Oh yes! I've heard about you. But why-"

"You have?"

"Oh, sure," she said.

"I saw you, yesterday at the bonfire, and today on the lake, you know, on the boat."

"Oh! I see!"

"Anyway, I heard there's a dance at the municipal building this Friday night. I was wondering if you could meet me there, or I could pick you up."

"Oh, can you hold a moment?" she asked.

"Sure," I told her.

Someone in the background asked, "What does he want?" and I could tell Jane then put her hand over the phone. There was talking but it was muffled so I couldn't understand it.

"Ok," she said a minute later.

"Great," I said. "You want me to pick you up or meet you there."

"No, I'll meet you there. Daddy will bring me. He says it starts at seven, so I'll meet you then. He says he'll pick me up at nine o'clock."

"Nine?" I said. "That's kind of early, don't you think?"

"It is, but I know he won't let me stay any later than that. Is that ok?"

"Actually," I said. "What are you doing tomorrow?" Today was Tuesday. Why should I wait until Friday to see her?"

"Well, we're going out of town, sorry, but we'll be back Friday afternoon," she said. "She you then, Danny."

"Ok. You remember what I look like, right?" I asked.

"Oh, sure. I'll see you then!"

I'd have to wait three more days to see her, and then we were leaving Sunday. Damn. What if she was as hot as I thought she was? I'd waste three days of potential heaven that's what.. And what was this bit with having to leave at nine? And why couldn't I walk her there and back to her place?   As far as I knew, everyone's was within easy walking distance of the municipal building.

For the next couple of days, we did the usual crap. More skiing, some volleyball, ate out.

Aunt Betty had asked me if I had talked to Jane.

"Sure, It's all set," I told her.

"Wonderful," she said. "You're such a nice young man."

I didn't get it.

Friday afternoon came. Ray Jr. said, "So you goin' out with Janey, huh?"

"Yeah."

"You're lucky, Danny," he said.

"How's that?" I asked.

"She's special. Ain't just anybody who can get her to go out with her."

"You're mother said she's shy. She doesn't seem too shy to me," I said.

"She usually is. I guess she just likes you."

"Yeah," I said.

After we ate dinner, it was time to go.

"Have a good time, Daniel," my old lady said, and she kissed me.

"Yeah, thanks, mom."

"You're a good boy."

Why was I such a great guy all of a sudden?

I got to the municipal building. A bunch of kids were milling around and arriving by foot. It was noisy inside already. A jukebox was playing 'Rock Around the Clock.'

I hung around outside for a while, and then peeked inside. I didn't recognize my girl.

Finally, a lone car pulled up in front of the building. There she was, sitting alongside her old man. She waved and smiled. I waved and smiled back.

I got close to the car window. My heart sank. She wasn't too good looking up close. In fact, she had pimples on her face. And her face was a bit chubby, too. I realized my imagination had gotten the better of me. But maybe from the neck down she was a looker. I opened the car door.

"Hi Danny," she said.

"Hi," I said back, and stuck my hand out for her to take it.

"That's ok, Danny. Daddy will get me."

Get me? I didn't know what she was talking about. Her old man was struggling with something in the trunk. I looked her over. She had a dress on. She was downright chubby in the midsection. She had huge hooters, though. Her legs were thin, which didn't make sense.

I looked towards the rear of the car. Her old man was pushing a wheelchair he'd apparently just finished setting up.

"Hello Daniel," he said, and he put his hand out.

"Hello, Mr. Melrose," I said, and took his hand.

"Thank you, young man," he said.

"Yes sir," I said.

Now I knew why Aunt Betty and my old lady had thought I was the best thing since sliced bread to ask old Jane out. This was going to be the last time I would let the imagination get the better of me. How stupid could I ever get?

Jane's old man and I carried her up the steps to the chair he had put at the entrance to the building. The place was pretty packed with kids and some adults. They were now playing Elvis. People were trying to dance to it, looking pretty stupid, if you ask me.

We went inside, and a minute later she yelled,

"Danny,"

"Yeah?"

"I'm sorry I can't dance with you."

"That's ok, really," I said. "I don't much like to anyway."

"You sure?" she asked.

"I'm sure."

"You like Elvis?"

"Nah. I like Sinatra a lot better," which was true.

"Me too," she said. "I think it's very romantic, that you think that."

I smiled and couldn't think of anything to say.

We kind of shot the shit for a while, and eventually my Timex said eight forty-five. In fifteen minutes, her old man would be showing up. And none too soon.

"Katie!" Jane yelled, all excited.

I looked into the face of a girl who brought goose bumps to my flesh, a tingling to my spine. She was that beautiful.

"Hi, Jane," she said. "Hi, Danny."

Did everybody around here know me?

Katie edged up real close to me. I could feel her breath in my ear.

"It's so wonderful you asked Jane here tonight. I was going to call you, Danny, but when you asked Jane, why I couldn't. She of course told me right away."

"What? You were going to ask me?"

"To the dance. We kept running into one another, so I figured I would ask if you wanted to come to the dance with me."

"Running into each other?"

"Oh, Danny, you didn't forget? At the bonfire and on the boat, silly."

Here was my mystery girl. My imagination had failed me all right. From the distance I'd seen her from, my imagination had fallen short. Real short. How I wanted to kiss those luscious lips just inches away from mine. And you've never seen such eyes.

"I've been keeping my eyes on you, Danny McTavish. But that's for another time. Maybe next yeahr. You'll come, won't you?"

"Next yeahr?" I gasped. "What about tomorrow?"

"We leave tomorrow, early. I'm sorry, Danny."

"You mean, all this week I could have been with you?"

"Well, not after you asked dear Jane. Now shhh, you pay attention to her! Bye bye."

She drifted away, and before she disappeared into the crowd, I got a glimpse of a gorgeous pair of legs below a short skirt. I had three hundred and sixty days to imagine what I could have done with the most beautiful girl in the world.

"She's pretty, isn't she Danny?" I heard Jane say.

"Were you with her on the boat the other day?" I asked.

"Uh huh. We always stick together, Katie and me. You thought I was her, all along, didn't you?" she asked.

I had a score to settle.

When I got back to the cabin, Ray Jr. was asleep in the upper bunk. I closed the bedroom door, went part way up the bunk ladder, and grabbed his pajama top with both hands, yanking him up from the bed.

"You son of a bitch!" I said.

"What?" he croaked. He tried to focus, and finally realized it was me in his face. "What, Danny?"

"You told me the girl who waved at me in the boat was Jane Melrose. But you knew it wasn't. You knew it was Katie, and Jane was driving.

He had come to. "Oh, yeah," he said, and a smile crept on his face.

"What do you mean, 'oh yeah'?"

"Just a trick. Poor Janey, nobody'd have asked her, if you hadn't."

"You bastard! Do you know how beautiful Katie is? I could have been with her all week!"

"What, and gotten in trouble with a girl all over again? I don't think so."

"Who do you think you are, you punk?" I yelled.

"Hey, you're chokin' me," he squealed. "You don't stop it, I'll scream!"

I let him go. I plopped into bed. Sometime later I fell asleep with the memory of Katie's face and figure and hot breath filling every corner of my troubled mind.

7

"So did you have a good time? Without me, I mean?" Ted asked.

"I had the worst time of my life," I answered. I could have lied, I guess. I could have told him I had the greatest time ever, insinuating that everything was just honky dory without his being around. But the fact of the matter was, I needed someone to hear about my sorry ass self being done in by a snot nosed cousin of ours.

That next morning after the dance, I told Ray Jr. to keep his mouth shut about the whole thing. I told him that if I ever heard that he'd talked to anyone about his mixing me up about who Katie was and who Jane was, I'd find him and kill him. When the folks asked me how the dance went, I told them that Jane and me had a swell time. So now my folks thought I was an ok kid, at least for the moment.

I told Ted what happened.

"That's too bad," he said.

"Yeah, too fuckin' bad," I said. I looked at the racks of his books along our bedroom wall.

"So what were you up to?" I asked. Not that I really cared.

"What was I up to? A new frontier," he said, real happy like.

"Really? You mean way out there?" I waved. "Different solar systems?"

"What?" he asked. It didn't look like he was paying attention to what I said.

"You said new frontiers just now. I figured you meant you and your pals were doing something with new kinds of rockets and crap, you know. Space shit, to go beyond our solar system, or whatever."

"Oh," he said, still kind of half paying attention. "No, nothing like that," he said. "A frontier you'll travel to someday."

"Me?"

"Yeah you."

"I don't know what you could be talking about," I said.

"I know you don't. But someday, when you grow up, you'll get there."

He was jerking me around, and I didn't like it. "Whoa, wait a minute. You sayin' you're all grownup or somethin'?"

"Just more grownup than you," he said.

"Just because you know about all that science crap and you do shit over at Princeton, doesn't make you any more grownup than me in my book," I said. "Yeah, you're sixteen, and I'm fourteen, but that ain't no big deal difference."

"I don't mean that," Ted said. "Look at you."

"Look at me?"

"You're immature for a fourteen yeahr old. I'm mature for a sixteen yeahr old. So there's a big difference between us. And you're brash, so you make careless decisions."

"I just have bad luck is all," I said. "Somebody's always out to get me."

"You see, that's your problem. You're always ready to blame everyone for the shit that happens to you except yourself," he said.

"That little shit Ray did me in. How was I supposed to know about that?"

"Did he? You shouldn't have trusted him. You have to consider your source of information. You could have asked Aunt Betty who the girl was you saw at the bonfire that night."

"She maybe didn't see her there," I said.

"Of course she saw her, or at least you could have described her. And you could have asked her what she knew about her, that sort of thing. You would have found out she's a cripple. It's part of the scientific method."

"What is?" I asked, totally lost. I was getting pissed off at him.

"Getting the right information."

"Well, it was your buddies who screwed me up big time with the science fair project. They're the ones who didn't put that sign on right. And they're graduate students.

"You're proving my point," Ted said. "You should never make yourself totally dependent on other people, if you can help it. If you didn't do a damn thing on that project, at least you should have made sure it was always in good working order, down to the finest detail. It doesn't matter if they screwed up, or you guys made it come loose. You always have to check."

He was making me ill. "Ok, ok, I get the point. But sometimes you have to have guts. Guts count for something too."

"What are you possibly talking about?" he asked.

"Like at the bowling alley. Calling a foul, I mean."

"Get off that," he said.

"Well, paying attention to detail doesn't do any good if you're not going to follow through."

"I've called some fouls, lately," he said. "It takes time to get used to it."

"Not against them IBEW types, you didn't. Like Kowalski, for instance."

"How come you speak like that, like a moron?" he asked.

"What?" I asked.

"You say words like 'them' instead of 'those'. That's how morons like Kowalski speak."

"Yeah, well, that's me, I guess," I said. "I'm just a moron."

"No, no you're not, Danny. You've got smart parents, and you've got me. That means something. But you always try to act like an idiot."

I stuck out my tongue.

He shook his head. "I'll tell you what," he said. "You're such a tough guy, let's switch places."

"When?"

"Saturday, or have you forgotten?"

I'd forgotten all right. The big annual tournament was this Saturday. "I can't. Dad won't let me call the line."

"We won't tell him. We'll just switch."

"Why would you do this? What's this really about?" I asked.

"I want you to start growing up. You're making the rest of our family look bad. You're going to be on the hot seat."

"You just want to see me get in trouble again, is all."

"Call them as you see them. How can you get in trouble? Just have the guts, like you said, to do what's right."

"You'll get yourself in trouble for letting me do this."

He waved me off. "I can take it. I'm putting my trust in you. Just be honest, and you won't get in trouble."

I was tossing an autographed ball in the air while listening to Ted's words, working them over in my mind. I glanced at the back of our closed bedroom door. I had taped to it ten pictures. The faces of nine Yankees were laid out like their positions in the field. Mick in center. Bauer in right. DiMaestri in left. Boyer at third. Kubek at short. Richardson at second. Skowron at first. Berra at catcher. Which reminded me of the fact I never did ask about what Kowalski had meant about bowling next season at Rizzuto and Berra's. Did they have their own bowling alley, I still wondered? At the pitcher postion I had taped Whitey Ford's picture, but over him I had taped a picture of me. It was small, and it showed me in my uniform throwing a pitch during a little league game.

In the hot seat. Yeah, I liked imagining being there for the big club someday, playing in front of the old man and old lady, and all those fans. Maybe even Ted would drop by the Stadium once in while.

Something was up with Ted. He just didn't seem like the same guy I'd left behind a week ago.

"Ok," I said. "What the hell. Let's try it. I wonder how Kowalski's going to take it."

"What?" Ted asked. I think he was day dreaming again.

"Me being on the foul line. Kowalski, you know, what he'll think of it."

"He probably won't notice," Ted said. "He probably even forgot about what happened."

"You kiddin? He's not the smartest guy in the world, but he couldn't have forgotten about it."

"Well, he shouldn't care."

"I'll bet you he fouls just to see what I'll do."

"No way. This tournament's too important to him," Ted said.

"How much does it pay, anyway?" I asked.

"It's a ten dollar entrance fee. There's sixty four guys. First place gets half, something like that. But it's not about the money with these guys. Kowalski wants to beat Snodgrass. Remember what happened last yeahr."

It wasn't a question, it was a statement. I was setting the pins on the championship lane. All Kowalski had needed was an eight to beat Snodgrass, and get a two thirty something. I'll never forget watching the ball as it came down the lane. Kowalski blew it. He completely missed his board at the toss. The ball crossed the one pin a foot in front of it. The ball missed the two and caught the four. Only six went down. Snodgrass began to hoot and holler, and for a moment I thought Kowalski was going to clock him one. It's a good thing he didn't, because one hell of a brawl would have happened, what with some of his IBEW buds looking on, and some of Snodgrass's there too.

Snodgrass had offered his hand, but jerko Kowalski wouldn't take it. He'd just ignored him and put his lovely ball away. "C'mon boys," I'd heard him say to his Neanderthal buddies of his.

"Yeah," I said. "You know, his kid was taken away by his mom after she'd found out he'd worked that night."

"Oh yeah?" Ted said. "Too bad."

"No it ain't," I said. "The kid's better off with his old lady, than that guy."

"No, I mean it's too bad his folks split up."

"Yeah, well, maybe," I said.

Saturday morning, the guys and me got together, and were playing ping-pong over at Lance's. It was a rainy day, so there was nothing much else to do. Lance's sister, Julie, was playing doubles with us. As much as I hated her company, she was a pretty good player, I had to admit. While we were knocking the ball around, I said, "We've got everything covered tonight for the big tournament tonight, fellas."

"We got the usual?" Jerry asked.

"You'll take seven and eight. Lance, you've got one and two, Sniffy's got three and four, and Ted's got five and six."

"Ted?" they both hollered. "What are you talking about?" Jerry asked. "Don't you mean you've got five and six?"

"You heard me right," I said. "I'm doing the foul line."

"You're shittin' me," Jerry said. "You mean your old man's going to break you in on tournament night?"

"No. It was Ted's idea."

"Ted?" Lance said. "So he's chickening out?"

"Nah, I don't think so. He kind of challenged me. He's been acting funny lately. I don't know what it is, but he's been saying some strange stuff. He hasn't been his usual asshole self since I got back from the lake."

"That's a nice thing to say about Teddy, Daniel," Julie piped up. "I'm going to ask your brother to marry me someday, you'll see. Except the thought of being in the same family as you makes my stomach turn. And for my children to call you uncle would be about too much to take."

"Don't worry your sorry-ass head about it," I shot back. Lance chuckled. "No way my brother would ever even date the likes of you."

"Oh yeah?" she said. "He likes me."

"He likes your mind, maybe, Julie, not your body," I said, and Lance and Jerry hooted at that one.

"He knows what's important!" she hollered, and chucked her paddle and I let it hit me in the shoulder. Lance returned the ball to me, and I slammed it hard off the table. It bounced up and hit her square in the face.

"You shit!" she said, and then she beat it.

We all kind of ignored it. Lance picked up the conversation, "What about your old man? Does he know about this?"

"Nah. Ted said he'll take the heat over it if the old man says something."

"He said that, huh?" Jerry said. "What's up with Ted, anyway? He's not being Mr. nice guy, he's just trying to get you in trouble, I'd say."

I shrugged. It didn't really matter. I was going to be in the hot seat for the biggest day of the yeahr at the old man's bowling alley.

We ate lunch, and the three of us headed over to the lanes. The tournament started at two. It was about a mile from where we lived. The highlight was walking on the railroad tracks on the way. We got a gas out of putting pennies on the rail, and if we could find them seeing how flattened they got after the train ran them over. Sometimes, kids even put old bikes on the track at a switch near a dead end. They ended up piling against the wall, all smashed up. We didn't do that though. I think we were afraid of de-railing the train, and then we'd really be up shit's creek.

It was still drizzling, and we tried to stay dry under our windbreakers, but the wet was winning out. The last thing we needed to be was soaking wet working at the lanes all those hours ahead. The tournament wouldn't end until after eight.

We came to a trestle and decided to stop for a bit and dry off. We took off our jackets and shook them.

"Maybe we should have caught a ride with your old lady, later," Lance said to me.

She was going to give Ted a ride, but we told her we wanted to walk. She'd drive us home, though, after working at the lanes herself.

"Nah," I said. I fished my spool and box of matches out from my pocket, which I'd wrapped in wax paper to keep dry. I sat on the gravel and leaned against the trestle wall. Lance and Jerry did the same across the tracks. I put a match in the spool, and pulled it back with the rubber band I had attached to one end of it. I let go. The match rubbed against the wood and struck and caught fire. It flew towards the guys. "We wouldn't be having so much fun," I added, dodging two fireballs coming at me.

"You know, I think this is going to be an epic day," Jerry said and grinned.

"How's that," I asked, sending another match away.

"I don't remember Kowalski ever winning, do you?"

Come to think of it, I don't think he'd ever won the tournament. In fact, last yeahr was the only yeahr I knew of he'd come close to winning.

"You're right," I said. "He must usually choke."

"Without handicaps, you'd think he'd at least come in second to Snoddy."

"He usually chokes too," I said. "It's the guys who you wouldn't expect to have a chance who usually win. The big guys can't handle the pressure, I guess."

I saw out of the corner of my eye a flash of light. A train was rounding the corner.

"Here she comes!" I shouted, and stood. We put some pennies on the rail and stepped back. I wondered what the conductor thought when he saw idiots like us doing that. Better pennies than bikes, I guess he figured.

The train roared by. I imagined getting slammed by it, and feeling my guts explode. I remembered there was some lady who lived around our town who decided to jump in front of a train on these tracks, and hearing about how her brains had to be scraped off the main street.

We looked for the pennies, but couldn't find them. We moved on, and made it to the lanes about one-thirty. The place was packed with bowlers. They were checking in at a card table. A buddy of my old man's was working it. The old man was ringing up a beer, smiling and yakking away. He had plenty to smile about. I figured he made more on all the drinks he'd sell today than the tournament fees.

In the back of my mind I began to wonder if this would be the last tournament. I pictured the place boarded up and dark because some guy had opened a new set of lanes nearby, with the new pinsetters. I heard they were opening new ones in Jersey all the time. Like uncle Ray had said, it was probably just a matter of time before it happened here, and the old man's lanes would be history.

The schedule was posted. The tournament was single elimination. A guy had to win six times to make it to the final match. There was a one-hour break after the third round, so the guys left could relax and get some chow. A lot of guys who were eliminated hung around to the end, and spectators always poured in after the break.

It was hot as hell in there. The old man had fans set up everywhere. The place sounded like a goddamn airport.

The pin boys took their positions. I looked at the empty chair against the wall to the right of lane one. I gulped. What would the old man say, if he noticed, or was told about me being there?

I took my seat, and the games began. After about one minute, I began to panic. I realized I couldn't look away, even for a goddamned second. Even if no one was approaching the line, I couldn't get myself to tear my eyes away from it.

How the hell did Ted do this, and sit here all night like he did? Maybe he could because he didn't care if anyone fouled. Or because he knew he was too chicken to worry about it too much.

But me, there was no way I would let myself miss a foul. I was a victim of my own determination. What if a guy fouled, I thought, and I didn't catch it, but Ted saw it? Shit, I'd never live that down. I didn't even have time to look at my Timex. I was worried about minutes and we still had hours and hours to go.

I wanted my old job back. I wanted to be on the shelf, hopping down, and farting around with the guys. But there was no way I could switch with Ted. There was no time. And there was no way I was going to admit to him his job sucked, and was somehow a terrific pain in the ass.

I started to reach for my soda pop, but was I kidding myself? We'd just fucking started maybe what, ten minutes ago? And when I'd catch Ted taking a swig, I'd felt like I wanted to bop him, so what would he think if he saw me drink already?

Hey, a guy down on lane, what was it, six, maybe slipped across the line. How could I call it when I wasn't sure? How the fuck were you expected to do this crummy job? No wonder Ted hardly ever called a foul; it was confusing as hell. And with all the goddamn noise and heat, I couldn't see straight, or think fast enough; the feet seemed all mixed together. I couldn't do it. I wanted to hear the old man pipe up, "Hey Danny, get the hell out of that chair!" but where the fuck was he?

I closed my eyes for a second. Fuck it. If I missed a foul, so what? It wouldn't be the end of the world, would it?

And maybe the foul I missed would be a guy who was bowling against Kowalski.

I took a swig. I shifted my eyes over to Ted. He hadn't seen it. He was yakking it up with old Sniffy, who was setting the pins next to him. Sniff'd been setting them up for sixty years, something like that. He told us stories when you worked next to him. I remember him telling me about the time when he was a kid in the Bronx, and a fire broke out at the bar, and it spread before anyone knew it. There was no way he was getting out the entrance. He said he looked up at the window behind him, which was propped open with a broomstick. He wasn't tall enough to jump up and grab the windowsill to get out. He told how the other pin boys had scrambled up and out, leaving him behind.

And then he said he saw a guy who was just his side of the smoke who spied him and the window. He said the guy ran down the lane and picked him up, and how he got out and fell into the back alley. Sniffy said he looked back and kept waiting for the guy to hoist himself up and out. He said he knows the guy was plenty tall enough to do it. But the guy never made it through, for some reason. Sniffy said he quit setting pins until years later, when he couldn't make a go at anything else.

There were no windows in the back at the old man's place. Just a side door, so it didn't matter how short you were.

I snapped out of it. Did I miss a foul? Or did I care? I took another swig. The root beer was already warm.

Finally, the first sixteen bowlers ended their play. I stood up and stretched. I looked over at Ted. He shrugged. What the hell did that mean? That he knew I'd missed fouls and didn't call any? I looked over at Jerry, who cupped his hand over his eyes and squinted. I guess he was making fun of me trying to see a foul.

I had half a notion of going over to Ted and telling him I wanted to trade places, when he pointed at me, and then himself, and shrugged again. So that was it. He was asking me if I wanted to trade. I shook my head no.

Ted had changed, there was no doubt about it. All of a sudden, he seemed like an okay guy, these past few weeks. It was as if he was trying to be my bigger brother, but not like an asshole kind of one.

What the hell had happened? There was no way I could say anything to him about it. I mean, what would I say, how come you're not such a shit anymore?

The next sixteen bowlers took their places. I looked up into the eyes of Kowalski. He hadn't even bowled yet, and here he was on lane one.

He stared at me, and gave me a grin like that grim reaper guy. He grunted, "Heh, you better watch yourself Danny boy."

"Yeah, I'll watch all right," I said. "Don't worry."

"You getting snotty on me, boy?"

I kept my mouth shut this time and looked away. I wouldn't give him the satisfaction of an answer.

Kowalski mowed down his first competitor. I was pretty much ignoring everyone else as far as watching the foul line was concerned. Keeping my eye on Kowalski was easy since he was so close. He didn't foul once.

The place was getting thick with smoke. My shirt was drenched with sweat. A fan was blowing behind each lane, but no air was coming my way.

The second round started. More spectators were coming in. The bar was filling up. I was happy my old lady was nowhere to be seen.

I started getting used to sighting along the line, watching more than a couple of feet sliding forward at the same time. I was pretty sure I could spot a foul all the way to lane eight.

The second round was half done. The high handicappers had to pair off against the lows, so Kowalski and Snodgrass wouldn't meet each other until the end if they both survived that long.

I spotted a foul, my first. I felt my heart skip a beat. I stood. "Foul on lane six," I yelled. The guy looked down at me and gave me the evil eye, but it was an easy call. I expected the old man to recognize my voice, but maybe he couldn't hear it over all the noise.

When the second round was finished, the sixteen bowlers left stood around the bar. Kowalski and Snodgrass were two of them. I heard the old man say, "It's five-thirty, men. Please be back by six-thirty for the third round."

I stood up. I felt stiff as a board and stretched. The bowlers were filing out. I joined the pin boys in front of the lanes.

"Hey boys," the old man said. "How about moving these fans up here to the front, and turn them around to blow out the front door. He opened it up. "Let's clear the air in here."

We pushed and turned them. Ted and I looked at each other. The old man didn't say a thing about me being on the foul line.

He opened the cash register and fished out some dough. He handed it to Ted. "Ted, take the boys to Angelo's," he said.

"Okay dad," Ted said.

"Have them back by quarter after."

"Sure dad."

The five of us entered the restaurant, and got a table. We were surrounded by bowlers, and some had their families with them.

Ted said what I knew he would. "You've called only one foul, Danny. I thought by now you'd called a million of them."

"Ok, I admit I may have missed some. But after a while I got the hang of it. If someone goes over, I can call it."

"What do you like better, Danny?" Lance asked.

"I like the action on the lane," I answered. "This sittin' in a chair the whole time just ain't my cup of tea. And it's hotter than hell up there in the corner. At least you guys have a fan blowing on you."

I felt a tap on my shoulder. I turned. It was one of the bowlers by the name of Cunningham. He was a good friend of the old man's. He was still in the tournament, but he was a long shot.

"Hey boys," he said.

"Hi Mr. Cunningham," we said.

"So what's with your dad letting you call the fouls tonight, Danny? Your first time, isn't it?" he said.

"Yes, sir. First time is right," I answered.

"Well, I guess your dad has a lot of confidence in you to let you learn during the tournament."

"Yeah, I guess so."

"You're doing a good job, Danny," he said, and put his hand on my shoulder.

"Gee, thanks, Mr. Cunningham," I said.

Cunningham walked away. "That was nice of him," Sniffy said.

We ordered pizza. After it came, I had my mouth full when I felt someone standing over me.

"Don't choke, Danny," I heard a voice say. "You don't want to bite off more than you can chew, you get my drift son?"

I looked up at Kowalski. I hadn't realized he was in the joint. He was tossing a toothpick back and forth in his mouth.

"See you boys back at the ranch," he added, and lumbered out, his big ass waddling back and forth.

"Nice guy," Lance said.

"I'd like to ram some pizza up where the sun don't shine on that guy," Sniffy said.
"There's always an ass or two like him in every town, and they usually end up hangin' around the local bowling alley. Make sure you don't end up working in one like me, lads."

"I don't think we'll have a choice, Sniffy," I said. "Automatic pinsetters are coming, haven't you heard? That'll be the end of my old man's lanes."

"Of course I know about 'em. They're expensive. They'll drive the price of bowling way up. So maybe they'll be a place for both kinds of alleys, with and without."

I hadn't thought about that, that the cost to bowl a game would go up. But I couldn't imagine the old lanes hanging around with the new. Things just didn't work that way. Hell, the old man's place wasn't even air-conditioned. I heard the new lanes had fancy looking ball returns and all, and cool air to keep people happy and probably bowling more games. You just couldn't compete with places like that. What did they say, out with the old, in with the new?

We finished and headed back to the lanes.

"You sure you don't want to switch?" Ted asked.

"No way," I answered. "I'm just getting the hang of it. You don't think I'd pass up the chance to call a Snodgrass, Kowalski match, do you?"

"Suit yourself," he said.

The sixteen bowlers left filled all eight lanes. Everyone else in the place was a spectator now, and more were coming in by the minute. I noticed my old lady had shown up.

Kowalski was on lane four. The guy he was playing against was keeping it close. People were packed behind his lane, and they cheered every time he threw the ball. But Kowalski closed him out in the ninth. Snodgrass won his game easily. I called one more foul, against a guy on lane three.

The tournament was down to eight now, so only four lanes were going to be used. The pin boys only needed to work one lane. I looked at my Timex; eight fifteen. I looked out towards the bar, and my old lady was staring at me. Before I had a chance to worry about what she thought of me doing the foul line, she gave me a smile and a wave. I smiled back. She had a bottle of Ballantine and a glass on a tray. She set them down on a table behind Kowalski's lane, and poured. She turned around and went back to the bar. I wondered if the old lady would tell the old man she saw me.

Kowalski destroyed his opponent, knocking down one strike after another on Ted's lane. Snodgrass was close to me on lane two. He was bowling lousy, but he still managed to squeak a win against Bender.

Now they were down to four bowlers. The old man always gave a fifteen-minute break at this point, so I joined the pin boys in the little shop my old man kept where he sold bowling balls and other stuff. They drew straws, which was the custom to see who stayed on. Sniffy and Lance pulled the two short ones. Ted and Jerry were to stay on.

"You want me to take Kowalksi, Jerry? Ted asked him.

"Sure, go ahead," he answered.

"I can't believe the old man hasn't said anything, Ted," I told him. "Mom saw me though."

"I think he's been too busy to notice."

"You think mom will tell him? I don't think so. What would be the point?"

"She smiled at me," I said.

"Yeah. That's mom," he said.

"Hi boys," we heard her say behind us.

"Hey mom," we both said.

"Hi Mrs. McTavish," the other guys said.

"So have you been calling fouls all day, Danny?" she asked.

"Yeah mom.   You gonna tell dad?"

"No. He hasn't said anything about it to me. He's very busy during these tournaments. But if you've come this far, well, I haven't heard of anyone complaining."

"Yeah," I said. "It ain't too bad."

"Well, you boys better get back to work," she said.

"Ok," I said.

The six of us were kind of crammed together in the store. I noticed Sniffy eyeing the old lady. He had about as much chance with a dame like her as I had bowling a three hundred. I kicked him in the leg.

"Ow!" he screamed.

"What?" my old lady said. "What's the matter, Sniffy?

"Oh, he's just upset he ain't callin' the next round, ma," I said.

The old lady looked Sniffy over. "You're not ok with it? Maybe Ted-"

"Ma, it's ok," I cut her off. "Let us get back to work, like you said."

We filed out and Sniffy gave me a dirty look. I bunched a fist in the pipsqueak's face. He then gave me a half toothless grin and said, "That wasn't much called for, lad."

"Up yours," I said. "Keep your goddamn eyeballs in their sockets, ok?"

The old lady turned around and looked at the both of us, and then walked away.

"See what you did you idiot?" I said.

"Runnin' your mouth, is what you did, son," he said and sniffed.

The bowlers were getting ready for their match. I took the chair.

Kowalski stayed hot. He was way ahead by the sixth. And then I caught his right foot slip across the line. I stood. "Foul, lane two," I hollered. Kowalski shot me a look, but I think he knew he did it, and he didn't say anything.

Also, he knew it shouldn't make any difference in the outcome. A couple of people applauded.

He won easily. Snodgrass was bowling better now, and won his match. But he didn't stand a chance unless things changed in the championship match.

The old man walked in front of the scorer's tables. He looked right at me for a moment, and then went on. I don't even know if he noticed it was me instead of Ted in the chair. He faced the crowd.

"Ladies and gentlemen. Thanks for coming here today as participants and spectators for the ninth annual McTavish Lanes tournament." There was some clapping. "I would like to introduce to you our finalists for this yeahr, nineteen fifty-seven's championship match. First, Mr. Bob Snodgrass." There was loud cheering and a few scattered boos. Snodgrass kind of half-assed bowed. The guy had as much class as a shit-faced boozer. His pants were cockeyed and his shirt was too, half hanging out. On the front of it, it said, "767 Series."

"And Mr. Harvey Kowalski." A few people clapped, but there were more boos. He was such a low life that he made Snodgrass look like a class act.

The old man looked at both guys, and said, "Ready, gentlemen?"

They both nodded. He tossed a coin in the air, and cupped it over his left wrist. He looked at Snodgrass and nodded. "Call it, Bob."

"Tails."

The old man took his hand away. "Heads," he said. He looked at Kowalski. "What'll it be, Harvey?"

Kowalski pointed a finger at Snodgrass, and the old man announced, "Mr. Snodgrass will bowl first."

I noticed Ted on the shelf, so I knew he had ended up with the long straw against Jerry, who sat nearby.

Snodgrass threw the first ball for a clean strike. It looked like he was heating up just in time. A bunch of applause broke out. I watched Kowalski get ready, and then I couldn't believe my eyes. Moving into chairs behind him were his kid and old lady. Christ, they must have gotten back together. The kid saw me right away, and mouthed a 'Hi Danny,' and gave me a little wave and smile. I didn't like this development one bit. An uneasy feeling ate at my stomach.

Kowalski placed his first ball way off, and he left three standing, but made the spare.

Snodgrass followed with another strike. It looked like he might bury the big guy. I couldn't imagine a better ending. Not only would it mean a loss for Kowalski, but a blowout would make my job a hell of a lot easier.

By the fifth, Kowalski trailed by sixteen, and then Snodgrass stumbled. He left two standing on his first ball in the sixth; a small split, the one four. On his second toss, he hit the one pin head on, which made it fly clear to the right of the four and leave it standing. A moan went up in the crowd.

Fuck. That's all I needed was a nail biter. What the hell was I doing up here, anyway? Man, there was no pressure setting'em up. And then I wondered if the old man would give Ted the extra dough for calling the line, if he hadn't known about the switch, that is. And if he did, if Ted would give me the difference.

But I couldn't worry about that now. Kowalski struck, and he gave a hop and a clap. His kid clapped. His old lady just stared straight ahead.

Snodgrass was getting rattled. He wiped his ball and tossed his towel. Kowalski took a seat and turned around to look at his kid and old lady. I think he smiled, if he was capable. His kid smiled back, but his old lady didn't. She just kept staring straight ahead. He took a swig of beer.

Snodgrass left the seven pin, and then picked up the spare. Kowalski followed with a strike, and took the lead into the ninth.

The place was packed to the gills. People behind the front row were trying to peek over shoulders and heads to get a look. I didn't see my old man or old lady.

Snodgrass spared and Kowalski struck again, which meant Snodgrass was now in deep shit. I was sure he needed to strike out in the tenth to give himself a chance.

Wouldn't you know it, the bum did just that. Three rolls in a row caught the pocket clean, and the crowd went nuts.

Kowalski needed to pick up pins, but I wasn't sure if he even needed a mark.

He wiped his ball, and set his feet. He moved forward and made his toss. He fouled, his foot clearly crossing the line. I froze. I heard the ball make contact with the pins, and saw Kowalski scream and jump. His kid jumped out of his seat, ran up to his old man, and gave him a hug. He'd obviously downed enough pins to win. He then tossed two more strikes.

Did he foul on purpose, daring me to call it? I never really figured out why I couldn't make the call. I always wanted to tell myself it was because of his kid, and how I couldn't steal his happiness. But another part of my mind kept telling me it was because I was just too goddamned chicken.

8

July 1, 1957

Dear Danny,

It was great to finally meet you at the dance. It's a shame we were not able to use the opportunities available to us to get together sooner. Oh well.

After I got back to our home, I received a phone call from dear Jane. She mentioned that she had a suspicion by things you said at the dance that you thought Jane was I. After she spoke to your aunt Betty, it became clear that after seeing me at the bonfire and on the boat, you indeed thought my name was Jane Melrose. How you came to that conclusion, only you know, I guess. Jane and I actually both laughed about it. And all's well that ends well, as they say, since because of your misunderstanding, you were able to give Jane a wonderful evening of your company that she would not otherwise have had.

I do hope that in your future visits to "the lake", you offer Jane your continued friendship. I know that she would like to get to know you better.

As for me, I shan't be seeing you again, I am so sorry to say. My father received a transfer in his company to another office to, can you believe it, San Diego, California! I guess I'll just become one of those worthless beach girls.

Just kidding. So anyway, daddy has put our summer place on the lake up for sale.

I hope all is well with you. Please give my love to all of your family.

Jane

I was fucked again.

9

After dinner one night, a bunch of us met down at the ball field. We had a game of six on six, and finished after the sun went down, and the lightening bugs were filling the air with their yellow flashes.

Me and Lance and Jerry hopped on our bikes carrying our baseball gear. We were headed to Jerry's for a sleepover, which meant that we'd leave the road at a dead end, and cut through the woods until we made it through to Jerry's street. That way, we cut off a good mile.

We coasted down the hill to the end of the road, and slid off our bikes. It was too steep and rough a climb from there to even think about riding, so we dragged our bikes along, huffing from the effort.

"Man, could I use some soda pop," Jerry said.

"Is it ice cold soda pop?" I asked.

"Yeah, so ice cold the glass is frosted."

"Good, I'll take one too," I said.

"Cut it out you guys," Lance said.

The woods were noisy from peepers and crickets, and maybe a few frogs. It was so thick I didn't think a breeze could ever reach here. We were almost dead from exhaustion; it was so stifling hot.

We made it to the top of the hill. In the distance we could see light from homes blinking between branches as we moved towards Jerry's street, maybe a half-mile away.

"Hey, what's that?" Lance asked.

Ahead and to the left of the trail were lights moving close to the ground.

"Dunno," Jerry answered.

"Let's go look," I said.

We stayed on the trail until it curved away from the lights, and then left our bikes. Soon after, we could hear voices.

"It's someone's backyard," Lance whispered.

"It's that kid's house, what's his name?" I said.

"Yeah, I know who you mean," Lance said. "I can't think of it either.'

"Allworth," Jerry said.

"Yeah, that's him," I said.

"Steve," Lance said.

"Nah, that's not it," said Jerry. "It's Sally."

We chuckled at that.

We edged closer and crouched behind a tree maybe twenty yards away from the voices.

"What the hell they doin'?" Jerry asked.

We could see two people carrying boxes. Suddenly, a light shined straight up from the ground, and a guy's head popped up. He put his hands up, and another guy handed him a box.

"Holy shit!" Lance said.

"What?" Jerry and I wondered.

"You know what the hell that is?" What they're doin'?" Lance said.

"Christ Lance," I said, "if you know what, tell us."

"They're fillin' up one a them bomb shelters!"

He had to be right. What else could explain what we were seeing? "I think you're on to something," I said.

"I ain't never seen one before," Jerry said.

"Of course you haven't, you idiot," I said. "How would you have? There ain't none around."

"That's just it," Lance said. "There could be, and plenty of them."

"What do you mean?" I asked.

"My old man was sayin' how some people been having them built in the night, so nobody knows they got one."

"Why would they do that?" Jerry asked. "I mean, why would they care?"

"Don't you get it?" I asked. "It's just like the Allworth's are doin' now. They don't want anybody to know they got one."

"Why not?"

"Tell, him, Lance."

"Look Jerry, if the bomb comes, the last thing you want if you got a shelter is for your neighbors who ain't got one to know you got one, see? Because it's for your family, and that's it. There's no room or supplies for anyone else buttin' in."

"Yeah," Jerry agreed.

"Hey, let's get the hell out of here," I said. "We've got some thinkin' to do."

"We do?" Jerry asked.

"You bet," I answered.

"What about?"

"I'll tell you when we get to your house," I said.

"Ok, here's the plan," I said, when we made it to Jerry's bedroom. "We gotta' break in."

"Break in?" Lance asked. "What for?"

"We need to break in because it would be fun for one. And two, because there's a ton of food in there, and probably soda pop too."

"So what?" Lance asked.

"So, just think, we can use it as a stopping point on the way to Jerry's and whatnot."

"You crazy Danny?" Lance said.

"Yeah, of course I'm crazy. But you already knew that, didn't you?"

"How we gonna' break in?" Lance asked. "It's supposed to survive a nuclear attack. How are we going to get in? It's got to be locked."

"Yeah, Danny," Jerry agreed. "How are we gonna'?"

"You're right, we can't. So we'll have somebody else do it for us. I say it's time we meet Leslie Allbright."

"Say, you just said his name!" Jerry said.

I shrugged. "It just came to me."

"Ain't Leslie supposed to be a girl's name?" Jerry asked.

"Yeah, but I guess it can be both," I said.

Nobody liked Leslie, because nobody knew him. And a kid nobody knew, is a kid nobody liked. If he didn't show himself around the neighborhood, he had to be a jerk. That's the way it worked. All we knew about him was he went to a private school, and that he was our age.

"What do you mean it's time we met him?" Jerry asked.

"How else are we going to get in?" I asked.

"You don't even know the guy!" Jerry said. "Why would he let us in?"

"Hey, I'm sure he's looking for friends, so you never know what he'll do," I said.

"Oh man, Danny, this just ain't worth it," Lance said. "And the guy's probably a complete jerk anyway. I mean, he never hangs out with any of us. Even his folks don't give anything out on Halloween. They're a bunch of hermits."

"We know their name, that counts for something," I said.

"Yeah, big deal. This is just trouble, is all," Lance said.

"I'm with Danny," Jerry said. "It would be a gas to see the inside of a bomb shelter. And we could tell all the other kids at school we've been in one."

"Yeah, and we could have a treasure hunt to see if they could find it," I said.

"You guys are both nuts, I'm telling you," Lance said.

"So how are we going to meet him, Danny?" Jerry asked. "We can't just knock on his door. I mean, we don't' want his parents to know we know him, do we?"

"Hey, I've got it," I said. "What if we go up to the kid, and just tell him we know about the bomb shelter and ask him if he would just show it to us."

"Yeah, and threaten him that if he doesn't we'll tell everyone else about it," Jerry said.

"That sounds good to me," I said.

"I don't want to have anything to do with this, guys," Lance said.

"Nobody said you had to," I told him. "But you'll be missing out."

"Missing out on nothing. Who cares about seeing what a stupid bomb shelter looks like, anyway?" Lance said.

"Well, they'll just be more for Jerry and me," I said.

"Yeah," Jerry said"

The next day, we went back into the woods where we'd hidden the night before.

"What are we hidin' out for, anyway?" Jerry asked, who decided to come.

"Look!" I said.

The porch door slammed shut, and Leslie himself walked into the backyard.

"Maybe he'll go in the shelter and we can follow him in," I said.

"You still haven't met him, Danny," Lance said.

"Shh," I said. "He'll hear us."

"He's comin' this way!" Lance said.

We dove for the ground, listening.

"Shit!" Jerry said, close to my ear. "He's still coming."

He crossed in front of us, and hit the path. He walked away in the direction we'd come from the ball field the night before.

"That was close," Lance said.

I raised myself up, and watched him disappear. "You guys stay here," I said.

"Where you goin' off to now?" Jerry asked.

"I want to check it out." I crouched low and scooted ahead. I was happy to see the entrance to the shelter was sort of hidden from the house by trees and low bushes. The door was even with the ground, set in cement. It was round and domed, like a garbage can top. There was a lock on it. I scrambled back to the boys.

"What did you find out?" Lance asked.

"That it's locked," I said.

"What did you expect?" Lance asked.

"Now what?" Jerry asked.

"I meet Leslie," I said.

"What about us two?" Jerry asked.

"We don't want to gang up on the kid. We have to make it seem natural. Let's go, I'll come back later and see if he's home."

I really didn't give a damn about the supplies inside the shelter. Hell, I just made that part up about using it as a stupid place to get grub on the way to and from Jerry's. I just wanted to see what the inside of one looked like. I didn't know how I was going to ask Leslie about it; I wasn't supposed to know they even had one. I guess I'd cross that bridge when I came to it.

Later that afternoon, I went up to the front door of the Allworth's house and rang the bell. The house was set way back from the road in deep shade. It was a perfect set-up to hide a bomb shelter.

A woman came to the door.

"Yes, may I help you?" she asked, in an accent.

"Hi, I'm Danny McTavish. I live down the street," I pointed. "I was wondering if Leslie was home."

"Leslie?" she asked. "You want Leslie? You, you know Leslie?"

"No, I mean I've seen him around. I just thought maybe I could meet him."

"Oh?" the broad said. "I see." She just stood there, not offering me to come inside. What the hell was her problem?

Just then, I saw Leslie coming out from a room in the back, and he spied me.

"Hey," I said.

"Hey," he said back. He came to the door and said, "It's ok, Elsa. He's a friend of mine." He was chomping on a sandwich. "C'mon in."

I went past Elsa who looked confused.

"This is Elsa," he said. "She doesn't understand English too well. She's staying with us for a while. From Sweden."

I got a better look at her. The dame wasn't half bad looking.

"Sorry," he said after she left. "I've seen you around."

"Sorry?" I asked.

"I mean, I'm not sure of your name."

"Oh, yeah, it's Danny McTavish."

"Danny."

"Yeah. I knew you were Leslie."

"I know, I heard you ask for me. You want to come up to my room?"

"Yeah, sure," I said.

The best way to know what a kid is like is by the things he keeps in his bedroom. I've got New York pennants on the walls, and Yankee pictures on the back of my door, like I said before. I have some of the balls and cards on display old lady Sweet had given me. Lance liked to build plastic models of World War Two crap, and displayed them on shelves. Jerry read every kind of comic there was, and his room had piles of them all over the place.

This kid had nothing, except a bed, a desk and chair, and a chest of drawers.

He sat on his bed, so I took the chair.

"So you go to private school, huh?" I said.

"Yeah, it's ok, except for one thing," he said.

"What's that?" I asked.

"It's an all boys school."

"Really," I said.

"Which reminds me," he said, "you want to see my collection?"

"Collection?" I asked.

"You'll have to get up," he said.

I stood, and he pushed the chair over to his closet. He opened the door and pushed the chair into the closet. He stood on the chair, and reached up and back on the top shelf. He came out holding a stack of magazines, and tossed them on the bed.

On the top was the July edition of Playboy. On the cover, was a picture of a broad on a sailboat. The feature story was 'Playboys' Yacht Party'. He picked it up and flopped to the centerfold, and held it up for me to see. Her name was Jean Jani.

"Not too bad, huh?" he said.

I liked this kid, with the girl's name. It's too bad we hadn't met before.

There was an address label to a Mr. James Allworth.

"My old man's a subscriber," he said.

"How do you end up with them?"

"After he reads them, he gives them to me."

"He does?" I asked. I found that hard to believe.

"Yeah, and he tells my mom that he tosses them out, so I have to hide them from her."

"No shit," I said. "You're old man's all right," I said.

"Yeah, my old man's an okay guy."

"How about you're old man, what's he like?" Leslie asked.

"He's like most, I guess."

"What's he do? For a living, I mean?" he asked.

"He has a bowling alley."

"Sure," he said. "I've seen it. McTavish Lanes."

"Yeah, you bowl?" I asked.

"Nah," he said. "I really don't dig sports. Hey, you want to come to a party?"

"A party?"

"Yeah, but don't tell anyone else about it, ok? Your friends or your parents even. I'm having some of my friends over. They'll be some girls there."

"When?" I asked.

"Tonight. My mom's out of town, and my dad said he's in some big meeting that will keep him in New York till midnight. Come on over just after dark, about eight thirty."

"Really?"

"Yeah, why not. You like girls, right?"

I hesitated so he asked, "What, you a homo or something?"

"Nah, nothing like that," I said. "I've had some bad experiences with them.

"Like what?"

I figured what the hell. I told him about Tina and her old man and old lady, and what happened up at the lake with Katie and Jane. He laughed like I thought he'd bust a gut.

"You know, you're ok, McTavish. We've got to get together more often."

"Yeah," I said. "Maybe I could use some help in the dame department."

"Just come by tonight."

After I got home, Lance asked on the phone, "So what happened?"

"I met him. He's real cool. You'll like him."

"What about the bomb shelter?"

I'd actually forgot all about it while I was with him to tell the truth. "I didn't bring it up. I will when I get to know him better. But guess what?"

"What?"

I told Lance about how his old man gave him Playboy magazines.

"Yeah?" he said.

"I'm not kiddin'. You'll see."

"Did you meet his old man?" Lance asked.

"No, he's at work, and his old lady is out of town. But this broad answered the door. Leslie says she's from Sweden. And she lives with them for some reason. She ain't bad looking, either," I said.

"Uh oh, here we go again. Danny falls in love," Lance said.

"No, she's old, like thirty something. And I told you I was finished with girls." Of course, I didn't mention about tonight's party, and about the chicks who were going to be there.

I hung up and dialed Jerry. "Jerry," I said, "you've got to do me a big favor."

"Yeah?" he asked.

"I'm going to sleep over at your place tonight."

"You are?"

"Yeah, but I won't get their until late, like eleven maybe. I'll throw some stones, or holler up to you when I come by."

"What are you up to now, Danny boy?"

I'll tell you someday, I promise."

"Oh boy, here we go again."

"Nah, it's nothing like that. Nothing bad," I said.

"Ok, see you later," he said.

I left the house about seven o'clock. I couldn't leave much later, or my folks would be suspicious. I always left right after dinner if I slept out.

I hung outside for a bit, and then realized I might as well snoop around the Allworth's backyard.

By the time I got there, my Timex said eight. It was dusky in the woods. I settled in the same hiding place as before, my eyes fixed on the spot I knew the bomb shelter to be.

I got antsy, so I crept on over towards it. When I got to within about ten yards, I came to a dead stop. A tiny bit of light was coming out from under the door, which was open just a tad. I cocked my ear. I thought I heard noises coming from it.

I slowly crept closer. I remembered Leslie's bedroom had two windows, which faced the backyard. I had to be careful.

I reached the door, but I didn't hear any noise. I know it was completely stupid to open the door, but I'm stupid, so I did, very slowly. It opened until the door pointed straight up and stopped. There was a ladder, and light was coming from somewhere off to the side of the bottom of the entrance tunnel. I quietly put my left foot on the top rung and started down. I heard heavy breathing. I couldn't help myself. I wanted to stop, so help me God, but I couldn't. I eased to the floor and turned around. I saw a room with two sets of bunk beds along the far wall, and shelves full of cartons of food. A guy and a broad had their backs to me, in front of one of the bunks. Their clothes had been ditched on the other bunk. She was bent over, with her hands on the bed, and he was standing behind her. They were both grunting away. I got a good enough look at the broad to recognize her. It was old Elsie, who didn't understand English much, but sure understood how to do the big nasty. I knew the guy had to be Leslie's old man, who was supposed to be in New York still. No wonder he gave his magazines away to his kid. Who needed pictures when you were getting the real thing?

I got the hell out of there as quickly as I could and still not make any noise. By then, my Timex said eight thirty. What perfect timing, detour included.

I went back into the woods, and out into the street. I made it up to the front door. There was plenty of noise coming from inside, so I invited myself in. By nine, everybody was there; three guys besides Leslie and me, and just two girls. The chicks weren't too bad looking. Leslie introduced me to all of them, and we shot the shit for a while. And then Leslie said, "Hey guys, c'mon outside."

We filed out the screen porch out back. "The real party's out here," he said.

It's dark out here, and buggy," one of the girls said.

"It's not outside, it's this way," Leslie said.

We followed him. Right towards the bomb shelter.

"Wait!" I cried, and hurried up to Leslie. "You can't," I whispered.

"What are you talking about, Danny?" he asked.

"You can't have it in there," I said.

He looked lost.

"In the bomb shelter!"

"How do you know about that?" he asked,

I told him how I happened to stumble on the guys putting food in the ground, so I knew it had to be a shelter.

"Isn't it supposed to be a secret?" I asked. "I don't think your folks would want anyone to know." I nodded in the direction of his friends.

"You're right, I guess," he said, putting his hand on my shoulder.

"Forget it, guys," he said. "It's too dark and buggy like you said, Carrie. Let's go."

When I left his place around ten, Leslie saw me to the door.

"Hey, see ya," he said. "Thanks for talking me out of showing them the shelter. I guess it was a stupid idea."

"Yeah, plus your old man might have come home early, you never know. Then you'd been up shit's creek."

He agreed, and closed the door behind me.

10

"Jerry," I yelled, "Jerry!"

"Yeah, I'm here," he said from his bedroom window.

"Let me in," I said.

"Ok," he said, and disappeared.

I went to the front door, and he let me in.

"Your folks still up?" I asked.

"Yeah," he whispered.

"Let's go up to your room," I said.

I plopped on his bed and sighed.

"What's the matter?" he asked.

"What a day," I answered.

"So did you meet this Leslie guy?" he asked.

"Yeah, you could say that," I said. I didn't know how much I should tell him.

"So what about the bomb shelter?" Jerry asked.

I filled him in about what happened just like I'd told Lance, but then went on about being invited to the party and why I couldn't come over any earlier.

"So we gonna see the bomb shelter someday?"

"Well no, not exactly."

"No? How come?"

"Well, I kind of already saw it," I said. I know I should have kept my trap shut, but I couldn't help myself.

"You did? How'd that happen?"

"Well, ah shit Jerry, if I tell you, you'll blab it all over the place."

"Tell what?"

"You know that broad I just told you about, that Elsie?"

"Yeah?"

"She was in there."

"She was? With you?"

"Yeah. No! I mean, I got their early, to the party I mean, so I hung out in the woods. Then I thought I heard something, so I got closer, and saw the door was open a bit, and some light was coming out."

"Yeah?"

"And so I went down the ladder and then I saw them."

"Who?" Jerry asked. "You said you were there with Elsie."

"Yeah, but so was Leslie's old man."

"I thought you said he was in New York."

"Yeah, I thought so too, until I saw the two of them, you know, together."

"Together. You mean really together?"

"Yeah, you got it."

"No kiddin' Danny. How'd they not see you?"

"They were standing, facing the other way."

'Oh," Jerry said. I think he was trying to imagine it. "Oh."

"Yeah, so I got out, and went to the party, and then Leslie took us all outside. He said the real party was out there in the back. He was leading us to the bomb shelter."

"No shit."

"Yeah, so I ran up to him, and told him the party couldn't be in there."

"What did he say then?"

"He wondered how I knew about it, so then I told him that I'd stumbled on the guys putting the stuff in, and then I told him how he shouldn't show his friends, you know, how it should be a secret, and he bought it."

"Wow, that was quick thinking. You think his old man was still down there?"

"I guess he must've been. He and Elsie weren't in the house."

"I say we go back and see if they're still in there," Jerry said.

"I say you're nuts. I'm not going back there for nothing."

"Well, it's not fair, you already got a look, and I want to see too."

"Jerry, forget about it. If they're still in there, they'll see you. They ain't going to still be, you know, looking the other way."

"How do you know?" Jerry asked.

"Jerry don't you know anything? How long you think that thing lasts?"

"Well, even if they saw me, what of it?" They don't know who I am."

I shook my head. Why the hell had I told him about the bomb shelter?

"Well, I'm going back."

"No, you're not."

"You can't stop me, Danny."

"Ok, go ahead. See what I care. Get caught."

"You mean that?" Jerry asked.

"What?"

"You know, about letting me go."

"You idiot, you just said I can't stop you."

"Ok, here I go then," he said. "You comin'?"

Of course not," I said.

"Ok, here I go. I'll be back soon," he said.

"Sure," I said. "Bye."

"Bye," he said.

He left the room, and I heard him go down the stairs. I'd thought he was bluffing, but he was on his way.

There was no way I'd let him go in that shelter.

I let him keep his head start, and went out the front door. About half way to Leslie's, I picked up the moving shape of Jerry in the darkness. I had to close the gap, so I started to walk as fast as I could without making the noise I'd make running.

The party was still going on in the house, so I knew Leslie's old man wasn't in the house. My Timex said ten forty, so Leslie figured he still had time to party. I went along the path in the woods. I came to the hiding spot, and looked towards the shelter. Just then, I saw the door open, and the light coming from inside lit Jerry's face. I'd screwed up by letting him get so far ahead.

He started to go down the ladder, and then his whole body disappeared. The idiot left the door wide open. If Leslie or any of his buddies noticed it, it would be all over for Leslie's old man. We were getting way in over our head. It was all my fault. I should never have gone inside the shelter. But then again, what was I thinking? Heck, if I hadn't, then Leslie would have seen his old man. We'd all have seen him. So I'd come out a hero. Except I couldn't leave well enough alone. I had to go ahead and tell Jerry. I should have known he would want to see for himself.

I heard a scream coming from inside the shelter, and it wasn't a guy's. My heart went to my throat.

Then I heard, "Who the hell are you?" I started to sweat like the dickens. What if Leslie's old man killed Jerry? I'm sure guys killed for less. Jerry was a goddamn witness to Leslie's old man's extracurricular activity.

I saw a head pop up. Jerry was then half way out when I heard Leslie's old man say, "Oh no you don't," and Jerry's body started to go back down. Holy shit, the guy had hold of him! But then Jerry started kicking I could tell, and then I heard, "You son of a bitch," and then Jerry was free. He flew out of there and ran like hell through the woods and along the path towards his house.

I saw the Leslie's old man's head pop up. He looked around and said, "Goddamn it." He looked towards the house, and he could see there was a party going on. He reached up and pulled the door closed.

I made it to Jerry's bedroom. He was lying on his bed, and he jumped up when he saw me. "Danny, where were you?"

"With you, you fucking idiot!"

"With me? You saw everything?"

"Yeah, I saw."

"He caught me," he said.

"I know, I saw you go back down the ladder, and then you kicked him."

We were both heaving for air, all out of breath.

"Yeah, and I got away."

"What did you see?" I asked.

"They were just sitting there on one of the bunks."

"With their clothes off?"

"No, with them on."

"Oh Christ man, he'd have killed you if you hadn't gotten away."

"No shit. Do me a favor, Danny, Don't let me be an idiot ever again."

"Forget it, " I said. "You're too much an idiot to ever stop being one."

"Yeah, maybe," he said.

We both laughed our asses off until we fell asleep.

11

A couple of days later I got a phone call from Leslie. "So did you have a good time at the party?" he asked.

"Yeah, sure did," I said.

"Good. Hey, my folks are having a barbecue for some of our friends, and they asked me if I wanted to invite a couple of my friends over. So I'm inviting you and Steve. You remember him, right?"

"Yeah, he's a cool guy. When is the barbecue?" I asked.

"It's a lunch on Saturday. Be here about noon. Can you come?"

"Sounds great," I told him.

So I was to formally be introduced to the Mr. and the Mrs. I wondered what she looked like, and if Elsie was going to be there.

Saturday came, and when I neared their house I saw cars in the driveway, and heard noise coming from the back. A trail of smoke rose behind and drifted into the trees further back.

I came to the front door and rang the bell. Elsie answered.

"Oh, hello," she said in her Swedish accent. "Come in."

"Hi Elsie," I said.

"Hello."

"I'm Danny, remember me?"

"Oh ya, I remember you," she answered. "Everybody is outside."

I followed her to the back porch, thinking about what she looked like without clothes on. I hadn't seen too much, seeing as Leslie's old man had been standing in the way.

The first person to notice me was Leslie's old man. He had a bottle of Schlitz in his left hand, and some snack in his right. Behind him was one of those brick barbecues built right into a brick porch. A bunch of adults were standing around, yakking and drinking. I wondered which one was the Mrs.

He turned to Leslie and said, "Leslie, one of your friends is here."

Leslie stopped talking to Steve and said, "Hey Danny."

"Hey."

"Dad, this is Danny McTavish"

He still had some food in his hand, so he put the rest of it in his mouth and stuck out his hand. "Hello Danny," he said with a full mouth. "Excuse the food."

"Hi Mr. Allworth. Glad to meet you," I said.

"Danny's told me about you."

"I hope it's not all bad," I chuckled.

"No, no, I hear you two hit it off swell the other day. Leslie told me that McTavish lanes is your dad's."

"That's right, sir. I sometimes work there, you know, setting up the pins."

"A pin boy, huh?" he said. "I don't think I ever mentioned it to my son here, that I did the same one summer."

"Really?" How'd you like it?" I asked.

"I had some interesting experiences, I'll say that much. You ever get hit?"

"Oh yeah, I thought I'd broken a rib once."

"I once took one in the nuts," he said.

"You did?" Leslie asked.

"Oh yeah," his old man said. "I haven't told you everything about my younger days, Leslie."

Yeah, and not everything about your older days, either, I thought. He put his hand on my shoulder and said, "One of these days we'll get down there and bowl a few games, Danny. It's about time we supported your father's business. But I haven't bowled since I was a kid around your age. Leslie, you'd like to do that, wouldn't you?"

He didn't look like he'd be too happy about it. "Oh sure, dad," he said.

"Good. Nice meeting you Danny."

"Likewise," I said.

After his old man started gabbing it up again with his buddies, I said to Leslie, "You don't have to do that. Don't feel like you guys have to bowl."

He shrugged. "It can't be that bad, can it?"

"You mean you've never bowled at all?" I asked.

"I don't remember ever doing it. Hell, maybe I'd nail you with a pin."

"Yeah, that would be a gas," I said.

I looked around, still wondering which broad was his old lady. A minute later, one came out of the house, carrying a tray. She noticed me looking at her, and came right over with it.

"You must be Danny," she said.

"Yes ma'am."

"Well, glad to meet you. I'm Leslie's mom."

"Oh, hi," I said.

"Would you like some dip?"

"Sure," I said. I scooped up some cheese-looking crap with a cracker, thinking about what could be wrong between Leslie's old man and old lady. She was damn good looking. She reminded me of those models you saw in those fashion magazines, tall and thin. Her hair was all dolled up in a bun. She wore one of those pairs of fancy glittery earrings that hang way down. I caught a whiff of heavenly perfume. She wore a real nice deep blue dress. She wasn't young like old Elsie, but I didn't think Elsie had a chance of looking half that good when she came to be the Mrs. age.

"Thanks," I said.

"Thank you for coming," she said. She left me and I felt shitty for her. But then a good feeling came over me. I knew my old man would never cheat on my old lady. They were too much in love, you could tell. And my dad was a mutt, and my old lady was a queen. I think he knew that. At least I hope he did.

Leslie's old man cooked up some burgers and hot dogs. Me and Leslie and Steve ate together at a table on the patio. I overheard the adults at the next table talking about rock and roll, and one of the guys was saying how it was bad for us young people. The broad next to him said she liked Elvis, and the one sitting next to her said she was all hot on Ricky Nelson. I liked his new song, 'A Teenager's

Romance.' I kind of liked his T.V. show, Ozzie and Harriett, but like I said before, we didn't own a set anymore, so I could only watch it at somebody else's place.

A couple of times I looked towards the bomb shelter, but it was hidden by bushes.

I guess you were supposed to have a radio on all the time so you could hear the civil defense warning siren in case the Russkies had sent an atomic bomb our way. I didn't know if there was any place nearby that had a siren. At school, we learned to duck and cover if the bomb was coming. What a laughable load of crap that idea was. We saw in a movie what the bomb did to buildings and trees. I didn't think hiding under a desk or making like a ball if you were outside would do you any good.

So what would happen if we did hear a siren? The Jennings would be in deep shit, that's what. If they made a beeline for their shelter, you could be sure as shit their guests would be diving in there right after them.

After we ate, we kids went upstairs to Leslie's room. We looked over his Playboy magazines, and I thought of his old man and Elsie. I wondered whether they'd someday get caught by Leslie or the Mrs. I knew I didn't want to be around if that happened.

My Timex said three thirty, so I figured I'd better scram.

"You want one of these?" Leslie asked me, nodding his head to the Playboy's on his bed.

"No thanks," I said. "There's no way I could hide it. My old lady would find it sooner or later."

I was working at the lanes that night starting at six-thirty. Jerry said he wanted to work, so he showed up then.

There were no leagues at this time of yeahr, so we had open bowling.

I was working lanes three and four, Jerry five and six. Sniffy took one and two, and Ted seven and eight.

We were on the back shelf, when Jerry said, "You know Danny, I ain't ever been that scared in all my life."

"What's that?"

"When Leslie's old man had me by the legs. Man, I'd never have gotten out of there alive if I hadn't been able to kick him away."

"I was over there today for a barbecue," I told him.

"You were?"

"Yeah, and I met his old lady. She ain't as pretty as mine, but she's damn pretty. She-holy shit, Jerry," I said.

"What?" he asked.

"They're here!"

Up at the counter was Leslie and his folks, along with Elsie.

"What?" Jerry asked.

"Don't you recognize them?" I asked.

He squinted, and said, "Holy shit."

"The old man said they'd show up someday after he'd found out from Leslie this place is my old man's."

"Why the hell did you let me work then, for Christ's sake?"

"Damn, I didn't think they'd come today."

"You think he'll recognize me?" Jerry asked.

"How the hell should I know? I wasn't in there with you."

"Oh man, Danny, he'd better not."

We watched them put bowling shoes on, and look for a ball while we set up pins.

"Please, don't let one of my lanes come open first," I heard Jerry say to himself.

The people on lane five had reached the tenth. When the first person finished, he took off his bowling shoes and put his regular ones on. "Looks like they're going to finish first, Jerry," I said.

Oh Danny, please don't let him recognize me."

Leslie's family came over to the lane, and put their balls on the rack. Leslie saw me and waved. I waved back. He poked his old man on the shoulder, who looked at me and waved too.

I was busy working my two lanes, and every once in a while I was able to get a look over on lane four. Leslie and the rest of them were the worst bowlers I'd ever seen. At least half the balls went in the gutter, so Jerry had an easy time of it.

"What do you think?" Jerry asked.

"I don't know. It's the both of them, you know."

"What do you mean?" he asked.

"She might recognize you too."

"Oh shit, I hadn't thought of that," Jerry said.

Just then I heard a scream. I looked up. Elsie had thrown her ball, but she wasn't screaming because of any pins she'd knocked down. She stood there at the line, staring down at Jerry.

"Uh oh, Jerry," I said. "You better look away."

"What the hell you think I'm doing?"

Elsie turned around, with her hands over her face. She took a seat, and took her hands away. She just stared straight ahead, like she was a zombie. I saw the Mr. and Mrs. go over to her and say something. She just shook her head.

"Help me Danny!" Jerry said.

"What the hell can I do? You put yourself in this mess."

A few minutes later, I saw Leslie's old man head to the men's room.

"Danny!" Jerry said.

"What?"

"She ain't bowlin'" It's the tenth. That Swedish broad won't bowl. She knows it's me."

"Settle down, man, They don't know who you are."

"They could ask you!"

I realized he was right. And also, that the old man might figure Jerry had told me the news about what he'd seen.

Leslie's old man came back, and threw the ball into the gutter. I was setting up pins, and I could tell something was wrong with Jerry on lane four. I looked over at him, and in his left hand was a small piece of paper. He pushed the ball back down the lane with his right. He stuffed the paper in his pocket. I knew he'd pulled it from one of the finger holes in the ball.

Leslie and his old lady finished up the tenth, and then they all picked up and left.

"Danny, I can't look at it," Jerry said.

"Don't," I said. "Save it for when we close down."

Ten o'clock came. The lanes closed down. All was quiet except the sounds of the old man cleaning the bar, and the old lady sweeping up. Sniffy sniffed, and headed home.

"C'mon," I said, and nodded towards the pro shop. We went inside.

"Ok Jerry, let's have a look."

He fished the paper out from his pocket and opened it up. Written in pencil was:

I know who you are. If I find out you ever told anyone about what you saw the other night, I'll break your fucking head.

James Allworth.

12

Jerry and I took a seat at the bar. The old man grabbed two cold root beers and cracked them open, then pushed them our way. The old lady was finishing her cleaning. Ted put a dustpan on the floor, and the old lady pushed dirt into it.

I heard the familiar cha-ching as the old man opened the cash register. He fished the bills and coins from the day's take.

"Fifty seven dollars and nineteen cents," he announced. "Not bad." He stuffed the dough into an envelope and slipped it into his shirt pocket.

Fifty-seven dollars away from starvation and not having a roof over his family's head. I guess it was a scary thought to have once in a while, but people kept bowling, so our life went on.

The old lady sat next to me. Ted leaned up against the bar. The old man offered the old lady a root beer.

"No thanks," she said. He shoved it over to Ted.

The old lady looked tired. I couldn't remember her looking so worn out. She rested her elbows on the bar and held her head.

"What's the matter, Barb?" the old man asked in the middle of finishing up a Schlitz.

"Just tired is all. I'll be okay."

The old man reached up to the T.V. and turned it on. I knew why he did it. The old lady needed cheering up, and one of her favorite shows was Ernie Kovacs. He turned the dial, and there was Ernie in his gorilla suit. I looked over at the old lady. Even though she was still holding her head, she managed a smile.

She sighed. "Danny," she said.

"Yeah mom?" I asked, and took another swig of soda pop.

"I think that's what you were meant to do. Be a comedian like that," she said, nodding her head to Ernie Kovacs. "You've got the mind for it. And I've always thought the most wonderful thing would be to make people laugh."

"I don't know mom," I said. "Seems like all I do is get people mad at me."

"You can turn that around, Danny. At least you get people to know how you stand. You always were that way. You know how to attract people's attention. That's the quality you need to be on stage."

Maybe she was on to something. Maybe that's what I was born to do, be an entertainer.

The monkey band came on and I heard the old lady give a chuckle, like she always did.

The old man put his elbows on the bar opposite the old lady. He said, "Hey Barb, you've got a birthday coming up. What do you say we go shopping for a new dress?"

"We'll see," she said, and smiled. A curl of hair fell in front of her left eye and she blew it away. It fell back down, and the old man reached over and lifted it out of the way.

"What do you mean, we'll see?" he asked. "I'm telling you I want to buy you a dress. When was the last time you got yourself some new clothes?"

She shrugged.

Just then the front door opened. We all turned to look. Shuffling in came Kowalski. He looked like he'd been drinking. His hair was wild and his head was a mass of sweat. He couldn't walk straight and he dragged his feet.

"What the hell brings you in here, Harvey?" the old man asked. "You know we're closed."

Kowalski waved him off. He eyed my old lady and slurred, "Hey Barb, Henry. Mind if I take a seat?" Before anyone could answer, he pulled up a stool and plopped his fat ass into it. "Just thought I'd come by and give you the news, case you haven't heard."

"What's that?" the old man asked.

"A friend of Snodgrass was in the tavern. Said one a them new shopping plazas is comin' to town. He says they bought the River Road Farm."

"Yeah, so?" the old man asked.

"Yeah, so he says he has it from reliable sources that there's gonna be one a them new bowlin' alleys with them new pin setters like we's been sayin's gonna come this way." He then got a crooked smile on his dumb ass face and looked at the old man. "Guess you 'n yurs is fucked."

I looked up at Ernie Kovacs. All of a sudden he didn't seem so funny anymore.

.

13

A few times every summer, my old lady would decide it was time to for us to spend an afternoon out in the country. She'd pack her picnic basket full of stuff to eat, and after church we'd hop into the Bel Air and ride west.

Her favorite spot was a grassy field by a stream some fifteen miles from town. The drive was through farm country, with plenty of wide-open spaces. The old man enjoyed the ride, because it gave him a chance to open up the engine, and "clean it out" as he'd say. We'd ramble by white picket fences, up and down and around hills.

The old man had checked out Kowalski's story early Sunday morning, and announced to us that everything he'd said was true. I guess the old lady needed to get away, because she told us right then and there that this would be a picnic Sunday.

We stopped along the way at an Esso station, and got some gas and cold soda pop. There was a brand there that the old lady especially liked, that she couldn't get anywhere else.

I watched her staring out the open front window as we passed by horse and vegetable farms. The wind blew her hair crazy like, but she didn't care. She seemed lost in thought.

We came to the dead end where we always turned left, but she said, "Henry, let's go this way for once. I'd like to see what's up this way."

"You sure?" he asked.

"Why not? We always go to the left. I want to go right this time."

I didn't know if she was looking for anything in particular that would suit her fancy, but we just kept on going, way past how far we'd have gone the other way. And then we came to a handwritten sign set on the ground by the roadside, which read,

Fruit and Vegetable Stand

Fresh Corn

Country Store

Feel Free to Just Stop By and Say Hello

And then just before we came to the place was another sign, which said,

For Sale

As we approached the place, the old lady said, "Henry, let's stop here."

"What are you talking about, Barb?" the old man asked.

"I want to stop, and maybe get some vegetables," she said.

"I thought we had vegetables-" the old man started to say.

"Stop the goddamn car!" the old lady hollered. We'd never heard her swear before, or at least I hadn't. And it took a lot for her to even raise her voice. "Please."

The old man looked as if he'd been slapped in the face, and pulled the car into the gravel parking lot.

A few other cars were there, and some people were inside buying and looking over stuff. We got out of the car, and went inside. The place had baskets full of different kinds of fruits and vegetables. On the floor was a huge box full of corn, and attached to it was a sign,

'Sweet Corn'

12c a dozen

There were aisles full of bottled stuff like jams and jellies and pickled this and pickled that, and corny souvenirs even, crap that no one in their right mind would ever want to get as a gift. The old lady looked it all over, and the three of us guys just sort of hung back, and kept our traps shut. She was in some sort of mood. But who could blame her? She'd just found out her husband's business was going to be history in a yeahr or so.

We followed her back outside, figuring she'd get in the car and we'd be on our way. But instead, she walked out back behind the stand, and so we followed her to the fields behind. Off to the right we saw the farmhouse and a small barn. She stopped and we heard her say, "Henry, I want this place." Then she turned around. Her face was lit with a joy that melted your heart. At that moment, the old lady just had to be the most beautiful woman in the world.

"But Barb, the old man said, "how would we pay for it? The bowling alley's not worth anything anymore," and he moved to touch her but she swiped his hand away.

"We'll keep it open until the last moment and save every penny till then. And our home is worth something, you said so yourself. And I have some money from my inheritance."

Inheritance. Were we loaded and I hadn't known it?

"Barb, you don't know anything about farming-" the old man tried to say

"We'll just have to learn, won't we?" she said. She spun back around to face the fields, and held her arms out as if to say it was already hers. I had to admit, the joint had a certain appeal. If we did buy it, I wouldn't have to wait until I was an adult to live the country life.

I figured I'd miss Lance and Jerry, but that was no big deal. They could come and visit once in a while, anyway. And I fancied that I'd get friendly with a cute farm girl or two. Yeah, I'd like that, lying in a field, chewing on a stalk of grass, looking up into the eyes of Daisy Mae, with the sun making her hair shine like gold.

14

It didn't take long to meet my Daisy Mae. In fact, it was about ten minutes. My old lady had gone back into the store, and found out from the lady working the cash register, that the owner of the place was a Mr. Worthy, who was presently inside the farmhouse. So the four of us traipsed to its front door, and my old lady knocked.

"Yes?" an old bag asked.

The old lady said, "I wonder if I might speak to Mr. Worthy. My name is Barbara McTavish."

The old bag looked the four of us over and said, "The store's over that way," pointing to the left.

"Yes, we know, ma'am," my old said, "You have a sign saying your farm is for sale, so-"

"Well, in that case, just a moment," the old bag cut in.

She shut the door, which I didn't think was too kindly, and a long minute later it opened. It was the old bag again. "He says to come in."

We entered a parlor, all five of us crowding awkward like just inside the front door.

"He's in the kitchen," the old bag said.

My old lady piped up, "Would you mind if my husband and I saw Mr. Worthy without the children?"

"Of course," the old bag said. I studied her skin. It was stretched so tight there was not a wrinkle, and was white as paper. I thought if you touched it, it would just slide off her body like dry bark. "You boys have a seat, if you'd like."

Ted and I followed her into a living room. There were two stuffed chairs and a sofa. They looked just like the ones in Mrs. Sweet's place. I went for one of the chairs, but the old bag said, "No sonny, that's my chair. You can have the couch."

So the three of us sat, and no one had anything to say. I mean, what could you say to someone like that? What day do you think you'll drop dead?

After about a minute, the old bag farted, and that got her going. I guess she figured that if she talked right after it, somehow Ted and me would think the fart was really her voice cranking up or something.

"So where are you boys from?" she asked.

"Trenton," Ted said.

"Ain't ever heard of a place like that," she said.

"How come your place is for sale?" Ted asked.

"Can't run it anymore, that's why," the old bag said. "I told Edward years ago to sell it, that this place got to be too much for us, but he wouldn't listen. The kids don't want it, so what the hell. Help ain't as reliable as it used to be no how."

"How many people work here?" Ted asked.

"Summer, maybe twenty five. Winter, just a few."

"Does it make money?" Ted asked. "I mean, my mother wants to buy your farm for-"

What the hell kind of question was that, I thought.

"What kind of question is that, young man?" the old bag asked. I laughed inside. "Sure it makes money, good money. Your mother will have to pay us for it too, can't go giving anything away. We started this place just after the depression..." but I had stopped listening. Tip toeing down the stairs was a fine pair of legs, and then short shorts, and then a beautiful looking rack, and then my Daisy Mae, topped with golden curls. I was shocked to see from the neck up she looked to be my age, at the most. What this girl would like over the next ten, no hell, twenty years, would be an interesting development to follow.

"Hi, grandma," she said, in a squeaky voice. She came over to the old bag and kissed her on the top of her head. When she bent over, the view of her behind set my blood to boil. I looked over at Ted, who was staring at me with a look of disgust. What the hell was up with him? Didn't he ever see what I saw?

The girl turned around and gave me the look over. "Hi," she said. She stuck out her hand. "I'm Molly."

I jumped up and took her hand. "I'm Danny," I said.

Ted stood, but didn't move. He just said, "Hi."

"You want to come outside and play?" she asked. "Do you have some time?"

Play? What the hell did she mean by that, I wondered. "Sure," I said. "Ted, "I'll be outside."

He waved.

Molly led me out a back door. We walked on an area covered with gravel, which became a path between two fields.

She hooked her thumbs on her short pockets. "So you folks thinkin' of buyin' the place?" she asked.

"Well, I dunno," I said. "We were supposed to be on a picnic, but my mom saw your sign, so she got interested, I guess."

"What's she want to buy it for, all of a sudden? Doesn't sound like you're farmers."

I told her about the bowling alley, and how it looked like we'd have to close it once the new one opened nearby.

"That's too bad," she said. "You think you'll like farmin'?"

"Me? I've never done it. I've never really ever been on one before. I don't think my mom has either. Guess it's something she wants to try. You know anything about it?" I asked.

"Sure," she said. "My folks don't want to have anything to do with it, but I like it, so I stay most of the summer on the farm. I can do it all."

"You can?" I asked.

"Sure," she said.

"If we buy it, will you teach me?"

"Sure, but there's a lot to it, you know."

"Like what?" I asked.

"You've got to know when to grow what, which fields to use, how many people you need to work it. Some things we don't make, like the jams and jellies, so you have to know where to get it, how much to pay."

"You know all that stuff?" I asked.

"I told you I did, didn't I?" she said. "I don't lie. You put your mind to it, if you have an interest in it, you can do it."

"Sounds like you'll be upset if you're grand folks sell it."

She shrugged. "I dunno. Maybe it's time to do something else."

"How old are you anyway?" I asked.

"I'll tell if you can catch me!" she yelled, and took off.

She went left into a field of standing corn, and disappeared.

"Hey!" I screamed, and tried to follow. She'd changed rows, which were way taller than me, so I could only hear her tearing through it. I stopped. "Hey, c'mon, I'll never find you." I didn't hear anything, and then I felt two hands poke me in the sides.

"Got ya!" she said, and I turned around scared as shit.

"Jees, you scared the shit out of me," I said.

"Take a guess," she said.

"At what?" I asked.

"You asked me how old I was. Guess."

Like I said, the girl had a body to die for, but she looked like she was twelve, so I said, "Thirteen."

"Close," she said. "I'm twelve."

"Oh yeah?"

"Yeah. You're probably wondering how I got these already, aren't you?" and before I knew it, she lifted her shirt over her chest, showing me her tits, and in a flash, sent it back down again, so fast that by the time my brain registered what I'd seen, her chest had already been covered back up.

"Geez," I said. "I-"

"It's because of my mom," she said. "She's got really big ones. She's talked about having them reduced, they can do such a thing, you know. I just wish mine would stay the way they are, don't you agree?"

"Yeah-"

"You think I'm crazy as a bugger, don't you?"

"No-"

"Ever kiss a girl before?"

"Well-"

She kissed me on the cheek and took off. She yelled from another row, "Catch me and you can see more!"

I started to run like hell, but I knew it was hopeless. I lost my breath right away, and sat down. The air was so hot and thick, it was hard to take in.

"Molly, c'mon, I give up. I'm lost, anyway," I said.

I heard stalks crunching, and then she appeared in front of me. I looked up into that gorgeous chest, which was still covered.

"Ok then, you lost." She stuck out a hand, and pulled me up like I was nothing. "Too bad, it might have been fun."

"What?" I asked. "You weren't serious, were you?"

"I don't lie, like I said. "You need to get in shape. Maybe if you come out here again this summer, after you buy the place, you'll get as good as me getting around."

"You do this with any other boys?" I asked.

"Nah, don't get yourself all worked up about it. I don't like a man getting jealous on me, now."

I followed her back into the house, my head spinning with possibilities. My old lady and old man were just finishing up. I introduced them to Molly, we said our goodbyes, and took off. I wondered when or if I'd ever see her again.

As it turned out, the old lady had struck a deal with old Mr. Worthy. They had agreed on a price, and she was to come back in two days with deposit money. She would pay a certain amount of dough each month, and when our house was sold after the bowling alley closed, the folks would buy the farm.

On the trip home, the old man wore a worried look on his face. Ted was being a downright asshole about it. He just couldn't see the sense of it.

"Mom," he said from the backseat, "you don't know anything about farming."

"Mr. Worthy will teach your father and I, so that by the time we close the alley and sell the house, we'll know everything there is to know about the farm. And it would do the both of you boys well to learn along with us. You've been such a big help with the bowling alley."

I wasn't about to tell them who my teacher was going to be, at least this summer. I wanted her for myself.

"So, you mean I should be a farmer, instead of a scientist, is that what you're saying?" Ted asked.

"No one is saying that Ted. But you'll both be expected to help. Just think how much you know about business, because of what you do at the bowling alley."

I didn't think that my pin setting did much of that, but, well, who knows, maybe she had a point.

"How come no one's asking me what I think?" I asked.

"Danny, what do you think?" my old lady asked.

"I think it's great, mom, I really do. I've always loved the country, anyway."

"That's the attitude we're looking for!" she said.

Ted shot me a dirty look, and turned away to stare out the window.

The old lady said with a smile, "Oh, it'll be wonderful Henry, don't you think?"

"I just wish you'd given it more thought, Barb, before signing that paper," he said.

"You know this is what I've always dreamed of having," she said.

The old man said nothing to that.

The old lady had won. In a yeahr or so, we'd be farmers.

15

The old lady was on cloud nine. She was full of humming and singing. Everything made her happy. Even when Ted started up again about what a crazy thing owning a farm was, she chirped about how he'd like it, he'd see, and how the country would do him good. Plus, she made the point that he'd be starting college next yeahr anyway, so what real difference did it make where we lived? And, he'd make new friends at school, stuff like that. And then he dropped a bomb.

"But mom, when I go to Princeton, if we still lived here, I was thinking I could stay home. Now, I won't be able to."

"I didn't know that was in your plans, Ted," she answered. "It always seemed by things you'd said to your father and I, that you were looking forward to being at school, working on projects."

"I kind of changed my mind," he said.

"Well Ted, you'll just have to grow up and live on campus," she said.

He sulked even more after that. He'd been in a permanently shitty mood since we'd been to the farm. All of a sudden, he'd returned to his old asshole self, only worse. If someone asked him something, he'd mostly grunt.

I told Jerry and Lance the news about the farm, of course.

"Does it have horses and shit?" Jerry asked.

"No, it's not that kind of farm," I told him.

"Then what is it?" he asked.

"It grows things that people eat. You know, corn and lettuce, crap like that. It's got a store even that sells all kinds of crap nobody needs."

"But none of you guys know how to do any of that shit," he said.

"Yeah, but they're going to teach us." And then I told the boys the best part. "Except I'm going to have my own private tutor, this summer, anyway."

"Who's that?" Lance asked.

I described Molly, and what she'd done in the cornfield, and how there was plenty of that stuff to come once I caught on to things.

"You're making that up," Lance said.

I raised my right hand and said, "Cross my heart and hope to die."

"How come stuff like that always happens to you, and never to us?" Lance asked.

"Lover boy, again!" Jerry said with a smile. "Some guys have all the luck."

"You better be careful," Lance said. "Her old man's probably got a shotgun. He won't give you a warning like Tina's old man, he finds out your fiddling with his daughter.

"It's her grandfather anyway, who's there. She just stays in the summer."

"Where's she live, then?" Lance asked.

"Don't know," I shrugged. "I didn't think to ask. Must not be too close, though, if she hangs around all summer."

We'll have to see this dame for ourselves," Lance said. "She really got nice titties?"

"They're burned into my mind, even though I saw them just for a flash. There aren't any prettier, anywhere, I can tell you that."

"She's got to be foolin' you, saying she'll let you see this and that," Lance said. "She just wants to torture you, is all."

I laughed at that. "You're just jealous. You'll see, she's a wild one."

"Maybe your old man won't have to close down his alley after all. Then what?" Jerry asked.

"It'll happen," I said. "I guess places like his is closin' all over the place, once them new ones come by. State of the art, they are."

"What's that mean?" Jerry asked.

"Just an expression. You can't fight progress. But I guess people will always need food, so we'll grow it so they can eat it."

"Must be real small schools out that way in Pennsy, huh?" Jerry asked.

"I guess. A lot smaller than around here, that's for sure."

"It'll be slim pickin's with the broads," Lance said.

"You only need one, if she's the right one," I said.

"What's your old man think about all this, anyway?" Jerry asked.

"He didn't have much choice. He'd had to look for something new to do anyway. I guess it'll make a decent buck. Plus, it's cheaper to live out that way, I think. It's real nice, if you like that sort of thing. And I hope to never see the insides of another bowling alley, once we close for good. They're just breeding grounds for assholes, you ask me."

"What, Sniffy ain't your type?" Jerry asked and poked me.

"Nah, it's not him, it's guys like, hell, you know who I mean. Kowalski and Snodgrass, all those league guys. They get on my nerves."

"I dunno, Danny," Lance said. "I think you'll be bored out of your skull. They got baseball teams out there, even?"

"Course they got baseball teams, what'd you think? Plus, I'll be able to play high school ball, for sure. Here, I'd be lucky to make the team."

"Yeah, you would, sport," Jerry said. "You're plenty good enough. Hell, you're the best there is around here."

"Our league, maybe. But only the best of the best of all the leagues around here make the high school team."

The next morning, the old lady took a trip to her bank to get the deposit money on the farm. It was Tuesday, right around eleven o'clock, when she said to me, "Danny, let's go." She knew Ted wouldn't go.

So we hopped in the car to bring the money to Mr. Worthy.

The next thing I knew, I was staring up at a ceiling. I lowered my gaze to see my right leg, propped up in a giant sling, all covered with bandages. I heard my old man's voice, "Thank God, Danny, you've come out of it."

I turned to his voice, and heard some movement. Coming to stand over me was Ted and he. I could tell from the look on their faces she was gone. They told me I'd been in a coma for five days, and so had missed Barbara O'Leary

McTavish's funeral. It was better that way. I wanted to remember her as I'd last seen her, with both hands on the wheel, wearing her summer dress, looking like sunshine...

16

The old man opened some soda pops and slid them over to Lance and Jerry and I. We gulped them down. He slid three more, and I held my hands over the ice-cold bottle.

It had been another stinking long day at the lanes. As much as the old man and I had grown to hate being there, it beat the emptiness we called home. The work helped to push memories away. The television was on to wrestling; anything but the Ernie Kovacs show.

The old man had been able to cancel the deal for the farm. I had told him I thought we should still buy it; that we should leave the city for the country life. And I told him I'd do as much as I could to help out with it. But he had no interest in it.

As for Ted, he was hardly ever around. If he didn't feel like working, the old man was okay with it. Until the old lady was gone, we hadn't realized how much she had been the boss. She had had a finger in all of our doings and goings on. The old man just hadn't had much practice at it.

What was the old man to do? He'd lost a wife and before long he'd lose his business. For now, he could keep busy running the lanes. But the day would come when he would have to decide what he would do after it was no more.

I couldn't wait until summer was over and I returned to school. I never thought I'd think that, but anything was better than being at home or down at the lanes.

So if I wasn't working, I tried to keep busy outdoors. I'd hang around at Jerry or Lance's place. I was too embarrassed ever to go back to Leslie's, even if I knew his old man was at work in the city. I had to figure his old man knew that Jerry had told me about the goings on that night in the bomb shelter, and I didn't want to face the guy again, or Elsie for that matter, who as far as I knew, had nothing to do but hang around their house.

I'd come out of the accident with a broken leg and some nasty cuts and bruises. The leg healed quicker than the doc had figured, but until it had healed enough to start work at the lanes again, I was stuck at the house, and usually by myself. The days had crawled by in terrible loneliness. Since we didn't have a television, I actually spent a lot of time reading Ted's books. I became a science fiction nut. I read books by Clarke and Bradbury and Heinlein.

Ted was gone most days. He'd leave the house with a see ya later and show up around dinnertime. A couple of times he wouldn't show up at all, and I'd ask the old man about it. He'd say Ted was staying over at a friend's. The fact of the matter was, I didn't know who Ted's friends were, unless, of course, you counted Tweedledum and Tweedledee, and that Steve guy.

Sniffy had taken it upon himself to help us out nights after the joint closed. He'd sweep up and help close the bar. The old man would give him some change, and he'd shuffle out into the dark.

And then Jerry asked the old man a question we'd all been avoiding, "Hey Mr. McTavish, do you know what you're gonna do after your place closes down?"

It caught the old man off guard. He took a swig of Schlitz and wiped his mouth, "Haven't thought about it, Jerry. Why, you got any ideas, son?"

"No, I was just wondering, is all."

"Well, you come up with something, you let me know."

"Yeah, sure. I will," Jerry said.

The next morning, I called the guys. I told them I needed to get away, and get some exercise.

"What'ya got in mind?" Jerry asked.

"A bike ride, and a good long one," I told him.

"Yeah? Your leg ready for it?" he asked.

It still felt a bit stiff, but I'd been taking short rides to help loosen it up. I figured it was time to give it and my lungs a good work out. I told the old man I'd be gone most of the day with the guys when he said, "Okay, but no sleeping over tonight. We've got Ted's award ceremony, remember?"

"Award ceremony?" I asked.

"Danny, don't you pay any attention to what people tell you, for God's sake?" He was edgy these days. I knew he hadn't told me about it, but there was no point in pushing it.

"Oh yeah, I forgot, sorry. I'll be back this afternoon some time."

I had the guys meet me at the ball field.

"So where do you want to go?" Lance asked.

"Just follow me," I told him. "We'll be pedaling hard."

I took us out of the city, along the road we'd take on our family picnics. After about an hour, we came to the Esso station and turned in.

"Man, I'm dyin' Danny, what's this all about?" Lance asked.

"C'mon, I'll buy you some sodas. We don't have too much more to go."

I went up to the counter. "Yup," the guy behind said.

"I'll have three cream sodas," I said.

"Cream sodas, what-" Lance started to say, but I waved him off.

"Hey, aren't you that kid I seen in here, what a month ago?" the guy asked me.

"Yeah, maybe," I said.

"Your mom, she orders these."

"Yeah," I answered, and plopped down two quarters. He popped the sodas and gave me my change.

Lance and Jerry took their drinks, giving me funny looks. We walked outside.

"Geez, Danny," Lance said, "how come you ordered these instead of cokes?"

"I just never had this stuff before. I just wanted to know what they tasted like."

"Ain't bad," Jerry said.

We gulped them down, even though we'd rather had the cokes.

"We going anywhere in particular?" Jerry asked.

"Yeah, It's an hour tops."

"What are we going to do for food?" he asked.

"I packed us some sandwiches," I said.

"You did? Really? Where?" Jerry asked.

"My lunch box is under my jacket," I said, and pointed to the rack behind the seat.

"How come you got it wrapped in a jacket?" Lance asked.

"Surprise, you'll see," I said.

We started up again. My Timex said ten thirty and already it was hot as blazes. A car would go by and pick the hotter air off the road and blast us with it. On either side of the road, the tall grass in the fields was standing still. My underwear was soaked and sticking to my ass.

In about a half an hour, we came to the place in the road where we'd turned right instead of left towards the Worthy farm. I went left.

"How much longer?" I heard Lance ask from behind me.

"Twenty minutes is all," I hollered.

"I'm dyin' of thirst already," he said.

"Yeah, don't worry, we'll be able to drink when we get there," I said.

My legs were burning, especially my right one, but it all felt good somehow. I stood up on my bike and looked up at the blue sky. I took a deep breath and blew it out and pumped harder.

I could tell I was leaving the guys behind. Finally, the gravel road was just ahead. I looked back. Lance and Jerry were way back, so I stopped and got off. A minute later they caught up.

"This is it," I said.

"What is it?" Lance asked.

"A place we used to come to."

"Who?"

"My family." I hopped back on the bike and started down the side road. The bikes slid some but it wasn't too bad. Before long, I saw the tree and pulled off. We biked over to its shade and ditched the bikes on the ground. I looked up at the branches. The last time I'd seen them, the old lady had been alongside.

"We'd go on picnics here, right under this tree," I said.

"So we're having a picnic?" Jerry asked.

"In a bit," I said and lied down on my back. The boys joined me. "You'll never believe where I'm going tonight," I said.

"Huh," Jerry grunted.

"To some award thing."

"Who's getting an award?" Jerry asked.

"Guess," I said.

"You?" he asked.

"Me? Why the hell would I get an award?"

"You said to ask."

"No, it ain't me, so guess again."

"Well, it's gotta be Ted then," Lance said.

"Yeah, Ted," I said.

"What'd he do now?" Jerry asked.

"Beats me. Must be something to do with Princeton, I guess," I said.

"How come he's so smart?" Jerry asked.

"You askin' that because I'm such a dumb ass?" I asked.

"Nah, you know what I mean. Science smart, that kind of shit."

"Somebody's gotta be, I guess. If Einstein had a brother, you never heard anything about him, did you?" I asked.

"Yeah, and maybe he's smart too, but just not that smart," Jerry said. "I wonder if Ted's as smart as Einstein."

"I don't think anybody's that smart, from what I hear," Lance said.

"What do you hear about Einstein?" I asked.

"Holy shit, ain't he at Princeton?" Jerry asked.

"I think he was," I said. "Only he's dead now."

"That's too bad," Jerry said, "'cause of if he wasn't, maybe he'd be there tonight."

"Einstein wouldn't have come for an award for some kid, you crazy?" I said. "He was much too famous for somethin' stupid like that."

"How come he got so famous?" Jerry asked. "I thought just actors and ball players and politicians got famous."

"You dope," Lance said. "That guy Einstein wrote that E equals some sort of crap, and it made him famous."

I laughed and said, "It's E equals MC. Squared I think."

"What's it mean, Danny?" Jerry asked.

"Can't say. But when he croaked a couple of years ago, Ted piped up about it. He told us he was upset he never got to meet him.

A breeze picked up, and the leaves made some noise. "I read some of Ted's books when I was laid up. One of 'em was 'I Robot'. It was pretty cool."

"Robots?" Jerry asked. "What did it say about 'em."

"It's about a broad, Susan Calvin. And there's these three laws for robots to follow. The first is that they won't hurt a human being, the second is that they'll obey the orders of a human being unless it's to harm another one, and the third is to protect itself unless it violates rule one and two. Anyway, the robots end up doing everything better than us humans."

"I guess you could say them new pinsetters is robots," Jerry said.

"Nah, pinsetters don't have a brain," I said. "The guy who wrote the book, Asimov, was writing about thinking robots."

"Yeah, well, not all machines are good. Them pinsetters will put your old man out of business," Jerry said.

"So," I said. "Machines do that all the time. They put the horse and buggy people out of business, but now how many people make and sell cars? I'll bet the people who own the new kind of lanes will make more money than the old man ever could. People will be able to bowl quicker. And they'll pay a lot more to do it."

"What if they don't want to pay that much?" Lance asked.

"They will. The new places are air conditioned, so people will like that and stay longer. And people will be making more money in the future, so they'll spend more. That's progress."

"So what do you think your old man's going to do?" Lance asked.

"Like he said last night, he doesn't know yet. He'll come up with something."

"Maybe he can work at the new bowling alley," Jerry said.

"He won't do that," I said. "A guy can't make much dough workin' like that. He's actually pretty handy with cars. He's always fixed ours. Maybe he'll open up a repair shop."

"That wouldn't be bad," Lance said. "Maybe he'll build you a hot rod."

"Yeah," Jerry said. "You could be like James Dean, a rebel without a cause."

"He's dead too," Lance said. "He cracked up-sorry Danny."

"Hey, let's eat," Jerry said.

"Good idea," I said. I got up and released the jacket and lunch box from the bike rack. I opened up the box and handed out the sandwiches. We wolfed down the peanut butter and jelly sandwiches.

"What'ya got in the jacket?" Jerry asked.

I reached into one of the pockets and came out with a bag of liquorices. I tossed a couple to the guys.

"Hey Danny, you ever climb this tree?" Jerry asked.

"Can't say I have."

"How come? This is a great tree to climb, looks to me. Must be forty feet high."

"I never thought about it, I guess. Maybe it's because Ted's not a climber. It does look mighty good though. Look at those branches. Even the ones at the top would hold us fine."

"Well, what are we waitin' for?" Lance said. "Boost me up." I locked my hands together. He put his right foot on them and pushed off, landing against the trunk of the tree with his left and with both arms hugged the lowest branch, and pulled up. Jerry did the same. "Help me up," I said. Jerry reached down, grabbed both my wrists, and pulled. I joined them on the branch. We scrambled up, and about halfway I took a left branch to their right. We stopped to rest. Even at this height, the branches were thick and easy to sit on. The breeze felt good against our sweat.

"Man, I'm thirsty," Lance said. "That peanut butter did me in."

"Damn, me too," Jerry said. "I thought you said not to worry about it, Danny."

"There's a water mill around the corner, over there, but you can't see it through the trees. You guys wanted to climb first, remember?"

"No kiddin', the water's good?" Jerry asked.

"Yeah, real good, and cold too," I said. "Last one up's a rotten egg!"

We dashed up. "Heck, I'm blocked," I said, maybe ten feet from the top.

"Hey, look!" Lance yelled.

I squinted to where he was pointing. I could see the sun reflecting off water.

"A lake!" Jerry said. "Did you know that was there?"

"No," I said. "We never drove down that way."

"Let's go!" Jerry hollered.

We bounded down, hopped on our bikes, and took off. The field dipped down a bit and after about a mile we came to a fence.

"Shit," Jerry said.

"Let's head back to the road," I said.

We followed the fence until we came to the gravel road, and saw it was gated. It swung open. I shrugged, "Ain't much use for a fence if you leave it unlocked."

"Maybe it's to keep things in, like animals," Lance said.

"Yeah, maybe," I said.

"We're animals, ain't we?" Jerry asked.

"Yeah, but we're goin' in, not out," Lance said.

We went inside the gate, and I swung it closed behind us. We biked down a hill thick with trees. We could see flashes of light between branches. The road turned away, so we took to the bumpy ground.

"Yippee!" Jerry yelled. He hit a rut and nearly bucked of his bike.

We cleared the trees and the ground leveled off. We ditched the bikes and ran into the water.

"Man, that's fuckin' freezin'! Lance yelled.

Jerry popped up from the bottom. "Man, that's cold."

"Must be spring water. I'll bet it connects underground to that mill I was talking about," I said.

"Think we can drink it?" Jerry asked.

"I don't see why not," I said. "It's probably better than what we drink at home."

We cupped the water and slurped it down. It looked clear against our hands.

"Hey look, horses, over there, through the trees. And they're drinking it too," Jerry said.

"And they probably drink it all the time, and they ain't died yet." Lance said.

"So Danny, you really have no idea what your brother did?" Jerry asked.

"Uh uh."

"He ever talk about satellites anymore?"

"Not when I'm around. In fact, he's not around too much anymore."

"Yeah, he hardly works at the bowling alley either," Jerry said. "How come? What's he up to? Buildin' a new kind

of atomic bomb or somethin'?"

"I don't know, but the old man pretty much lets him do whatever he wants. My mom wouldn't have let him do that. I guess she was the boss, but we didn't know it, if you know what I mean."

"Ain't too many ladies around who were as pretty as she was, Danny," Jerry said.

"Shut up, Jerry, don't you think Danny knows that?" Lance said.

"Hey, some people on horses," Jerry said.

Two horses with riders were coming to the edge of the lake to join the other two. We watched them bend their heads down to drink. I squinted. It couldn't be.

"Holy cow," I said to myself.

"Holy cow, what?" Lance asked.

"It's Molly, c'mon!" I yelled.

I swam as fast as I could to shallow water, and ran the rest of the way to the riverbank. We hopped on the bikes and rode.

"Danny, that you?" Molly called when she recognized me.

"Hi Molly," I said and broke to a stop. She jumped down from her horse and gave me a big squeeze. Her boobs pressed against me. She pulled away and said, "Oh Danny, I'm so sorry. I feel like we're responsible in some way."

"Nah, c'mon," was all I could think to say.

"This is my cousin, Kevin," she said.

"Hey," I said. He looked to be about ten. "These are my buddies Jerry and Lance."

"Hi fellas," Holly said. "What are you doin' out this way, Danny?"

"My family used to picnic up that way. We rode our bikes in when we saw the lake from a tree. Ain't you kinda far yourself?"

"Not really. Maybe a half hour ride goin' easy," she said. "I go home tomorrow Danny."

"I never did ask you where that is," I said.

"I live in California. I don't like it much in the summer. It's nasty where we live around San Francisco."

Another California girl, who would come and go from my life, I thought.

"But I'll be back again next summer. We can get together then. Your dad, he wasn't much interested in the farm, huh?"

"No, I knew that. My mom had persuaded him to buy it. Anyway, you won't be coming back if it sells before then."

"I suppose you're right," she said.

I knew I'd never see her again. But I never expected to anyway before just now. My Timex said near one. "Well, maybe we'd best be goin' I guess," I said.

"If you've got some time, why don't you boys come back to the farm with us?" Molly asked.

"I dunno. We got our bikes."

"Leave 'em here," she said. "Gramp can drive you back here in his truck and drive you home. We're havin' a big cookout. We always do my last day. All the help comes and we close early for it. Gramp and grandma will be glad to see you, I know it."

"How we gonna get there, run?" Lance asked.

"That's easy," Kevin piped up. "We got these two horses. Molly, we can put two of 'em on Teresa, and put the other guy on Missy."

"What do you say boys?" Molly asked.

"I ain't ever been on a horse before," Jerry said. He looked scared.

"Well hell, I ain't either," I said. "Lance you ever been?"

He shook his head. "We can try, but these two ain't even saddled."

"He's got a point Kevin," Molly said.

Kevin said, "I can go bareback, that ain't no problem. Why doesn't your friend Danny go with you, and the other two can hop on Spider."

So there I ended up, scrunched tight behind Molly. I put my arms around her waist, figuring once in a while could slip them up to her chest if things got bouncy. I buried my snout into that thick blond hair of hers. It smelled downright nice.

It took a while for Kevin to get Jerry and Lance situated into the other saddle, and he led them by the rein from his horse.

We didn't get far and Lance hooted, "Shit, my ass and legs are killin' me. How far we got to go?"

I felt like I would split in two myself, but I was damned if I would complain about it.

"We'll be there in forty-five minutes or so," Molly said. "Maybe an hour by the look of things. Too bad you boys can't ride, we'd be there in half that time. How you doin' back there sport?"

"Swell," I answered. "Is this how people get bow legged?"

"You bet," she laughed. If Molly wasn't so good looking, I'd have wanted to get the hell off and maybe smack her one for putting me through this. But since she was, I laughed and thought she was funny.

We went by road most of the way, and cut through fields whenever we could which I figured must be shortcuts. Whenever we went downhill, I thought our horse would slip and I'd fall off and get crushed to death underneath it.

"Christ, we're gonna fall," I heard Jerry say.

"No we ain't," Lance told him. "Horses know how to go downhill, they have to do it all the time."

About an hour later, we came to a ridge, and the farm was just below. The road we'd come in on that day was on the other side.

"Damn, this is too steep," Jerry said. "Let me get off, I'll walk from here."

"Yeah, me too," Lance said. "My ass and legs have had enough."

Kevin helped them off.

"You want off too?" Molly asked me. I realized I'd completely forgotten about trying to get a feel of her titties, I'd been so caught up in the ride, aching like hell.

"Nah, I'm okay," I lied. I was determined to slip my hands up on the way down the hill.

We started with Kevin now on the other saddled horse. The boys ran a bit ahead. Kevin was in front of us, so no one would see me.

It was a bumpy ride, and I tried to slide my hands up a bit, but they jerked up instead, and I hit her chest awkward like.

"Danny don't be so rough," Molly said. "And if you're gonna do that, put your hands under my shirt, stupid."

"Do what?" I asked.

"Oh c'mon now. I know you're trying to get a feel. I showed 'em to you. The least I can do is let you touch them."

"Okay," I said. I put my hands against her belly and moved them up until I found the bottom of her tits.

"Higher Danny," she said.

"I moved my hands slowly up and onto those delicious mounds. I felt her nipples. The whole deal was bigger and heavier than I'd imagined.

"Ya like 'em?" she asked.

I took my hands away.

You don't like them Danny?"

"I, yeah, I like them fine," I said.

"Then, why did you take your hands away?" she asked.

"I don't know, Molly. It just doesn't seem right."

"That's okay," she said. "You see, that's why I don't have a boyfriend.

"What do you mean?" I asked.

"Back home, it's the same thing. I scare the boys away that are our age. And I'm too young for the older ones. You see what I mean?"

"Yeah, maybe," I said. "Molly, you're too much."

"I know," she said. "I'm a little girl in a big girl's body."

"I didn't mean it that way," I told her. "Molly, you'll come back next summer, won't you?"

"I will if the farm doesn't sell. You're not falling in love with me Danny, are you?"

I smelled her hair. I was, I think. "Yeah, I think I am."

"Puppy love, they call it. Or maybe it's titty love, you know. Trouble is, I come back next yeahr, I might be too big already. Remember I told you about my mom?"

I was feeling hot, but from deep inside. I was kind of dizzy my mind was so loused up.

We came to the farm and got off the horse. My legs felt wobbly.

"You okay, Danny?" Jerry asked. "You don't look so good."

"He's okay," Molly said. "He just needs somethin' cold, is all. You boys look like you could use a drink too."

"You better believe it," Lance said.

Just behind the farmhouse were five picnic tables, one of them with a spread of food. A couple of metal tubs were filled with ice. Soda and beer bottles were mixed in with it. About twenty people were standing around, most with a bottle in their hand.

"What's that thing they're using as a barbecue?" Jerry asked.

"It's a couple of oil drums," Molly said. "Gramp makes 'em into smokers. He's got ribs and chicken in there."

Old bag Worthy was sitting in a lawn chair, swigging on a beer. Old man Worthy was shooting the shit with some of the help.

Molly brought us over to them. "Gramp, grandma, you remember Danny McTavish, don't you? He and his friends were nearby, so me and Kevin brought them here for the barbecue."

Old man Worthy stuck out his hand. His fingers looked like bratwursts. "Danny," he said.

"Hi Mr. Worthy."

"The Missus and I extend our sincerest condolences. I heard you were injured. How are you?"

"Okay. I broke my leg and got scratched up a bit, but I'm doing fine, thanks."

I looked down at the old bag. She smiled.

"Hi Mrs. Worthy," I said.

"Hello, young man. Who are your friends?"

"This is Lance and Jerry."

"It's nice to see you boys. Hungry?"

"Yes ma'am," we all said.

"Well, that's fine," she said. She looked at the boys and said, "Your friend here got an early lunch in a manner of speaking."

"Yeah, we ate a peanut butter and jelly sandwich he packed," Lance said. "But we're hungry just the same."

"No, I didn't mean that," she said. She stared at Molly as she said it. She reached down and picked up a pair of binoculars. She looked at me and smiled again. "I don't miss much around here, sonny boy."

I looked at Molly, which was stupid. I might as well have said, "Yeah, she sure has great tits."

"Grandma, you imagining things now?" Molly asked.

"You'd better learn to keep some things to yourself, my little darling," she said. "If you don't, things have a way of getting out of hand, if you catch my meaning."

Me and the boys walked away, and Lance asked, "What was that lady talkin' about, Danny?"

"What did you do now?" Jerry asked and laughed.

"It was her titties, wasn't it?" Lance asked.

"Sort of," I said.

"You feel 'em?" Lance asked.

"I can't believe the old bag saw me. I slipped my hands under Molly's shirt. She told me to do it."

"No shit!" Lance said.

"Yeah, and they're nice all right," I said.

"And that old bag saw you through the binoculars?"

"I guess so," I said.

"Ain't that somethin'", Jerry said. "Guess she ain't got nothin' better to do."

"C'mon guys," Molly called to us. "Food's ready."

We entered a food line behind Molly and Kevin.

"Hey Molly, thanks for inviting us," Jerry said. "Man, they got everything here."

"Pretty much everybody makes a dish. You gotta try those baked beans with bacon," Molly said.

"My favorite is what that fella makes your always showing your titties to," Kevin said.

Molly slapped him.

"Hey, it's true," Kevin said. "You let Danny feel 'em, didn't you? That's what granny was talkin' about, wasn't she?"

"You mind your mouth, kiddo," Molly said. "Don't mind him," Molly said to me. "He just makes stuff up."

"Yeah," I said.

"You still love me, don't you Danny?" she asked.

I looked at Jerry and Lance. Jerry grew a big smile on his face.

"Uh, I dunno," I said.

"It's okay, Danny," Molly said. "You can admit it in front of your friends."

"Don't go sayin' it, Danny," Kevin said. "Every guy around here falls in love with Molly, and it's her titties they's fall in love with."

"Why you," Molly said, and slammed Kevin with a haymaker. He went down, holding onto his right cheek. "You stay down, you punk," she said, and kicked him.

"Exhibitionist," he said.

"Shut up," she said, and tried to kick him again but he dodged her foot.

"What's going on here, you're holding up the line," one of the guys serving the food said.

Kevin had stood back up. His cheek had a big red welt on it. He gave Molly a dark look.

"I'm glad you're going back to Caleefornia tomorrow," he said, and walked away.

By now I'd lost my appetite, for both food and women. I picked at my plate, while the guys slobbered theirs down. We just sort of hung around for a few more hours. Molly and I didn't say much of anything to each other. My Timex said a quarter to four, and she eventually asked old man Worthy if he could give us a ride.

By the time he drove us to the ball field, it was nearly five o'clock. The guys had ridden in the back of the truck, while I sat next to the old man. When we stopped, he said to me, "Get her out of your mind, son. I know what it's like to have a fire lit under you when you're young. Farm 'll probably be sold by next summer anyway."

He didn't have to say it. When Molly and I had said our goodbyes, I had no interest in seeing her ever again.

17

"You can't wear that," Ted said.

"How come?" I asked.

"Because you have to look nice, that's why," he answered.

"Says who?" I asked.

"Says me. You have to wear a jacket and tie. It's mandatory. You can't go looking like an idiot to my award ceremony."

"Since when does wearing a nice shirt like I got on make me look like an idiot?" I pointed out. I was getting hot. I didn't need Ted bossing me around, especially this new Ted who was hardly ever home.

"This award is important to me, Danny. I'll be damned if you're going to screw it up."

"Screw it up? What's what I'm wearing got anything to do with screwing up your award? What's it for anyway?" I asked. "You invent some kinda new gizmo or something?"

"You not only dress like a slob," he said, "you are a slob. You're always leaving my books lying around. Is that supposed to impress me, to make me think you're actually reading them?"

"I am reading them, sure as shit," I said. "Ask me the three laws of a robot."

"No."

"Go ahead, you're chicken."

"So you're trying to tell me you've actually been reading? Danny the scientist."

"Yeah, how about that? You ain't the only smart one around here."

"Good, if you're so smart, act it. You can start by putting on a jacket and tie. If you don't believe you have to, ask dad."

I did ask him, and he told me I had to wear a jacket and tie. I tried, but all the collars on my shirts were way too small to button around my neck.

"Look," I told Ted. "Every shirt's like this," I showed him. "There's no way I can button the collar."

"When was the last time you wore a tie?" he asked.

I shrugged. I supposed everybody did at the old lady's funeral, but I had missed it.

"You'll just have to wear one of my shirts, then," he said.

So I went to the stupid award thing with this gigantic collar and cuffs I had to keep pushing back from my palms. Now I did look like an idiot, and it was all Ted's fault.

I hopped in the backseat of the Bel Air. It was nearly dark, and the lights on the side of the highway threw shafts of light against the car, so it looked like they were pushing us forward as we moved past them. On the radio, Dean Martin was singing 'Write to me from Naples'. The old lady would have been singing it right now if she was sitting in the front seat instead of Ted.

I looked at the back of his head. I imagined the old lady's, and her long curly brown hair. I imagined the smell of her perfume. I felt a lump in my throat coming on. I hated that feeling more than anything.

Ted won a regional award for excellence in science, which qualified him to compete on a national level. It was a night I won't ever forget.

18

The next morning, I woke with a purpose for the first time in my life. I was determined to make the woman I'd met the night before my new mother.

You might ask how I could think such a thing, so close to the death of my own. How I could ask a stranger to be everything the old lady had been and meant to me.

Of course, she couldn't be; no one could. But I was lost and empty, without a woman in the house who talked, laughed, sang, and bossed me around as only a woman can do.

And my old man was lost, too. Oh sure, it would take some time, but I would do whatever it took to convince the old man, Henry McTavish, to hitch up with Miss Jeannie.

And Ted was the key. You see, Miss Jeannie had been Ted's junior yeahr science teacher, and she had showed up at the ceremony to see her prize pupil receive his award. Ted didn't sit with us, so as it turned out, I sat between the old man and she. Miss Jeannie had recognized the old man, and asked if she could join us. Of course the old man had obliged. In thinking about it later, I should have made sure he sat next to her, but it didn't happen that way.

Miss Jeannie was a complete knockout. She wore a simple, black dress, which came down to her ankles, and she her figure filled it perfectly. And, she was a stunner. She had a different look than my old lady, but she was no less beautiful. Her voice was quiet and sweet, so that her words sounded as if she was telling you a secret. She breathed them, so you could feel them to the center of your heart. And the air around her smelled of something fresh and clean, so that it was as if she carried you away with her into a private world of just two.

I guessed she was in her early thirties. The old man was thirty-seven, so they were a good match, age wise.

When the ceremony ended, everybody gathered in a lobby for drinks and snacks. The three of us found Ted. When he saw Miss Jeannie, his face dropped to the floor.

"I, I didn't know you were coming, Miss Sullivan," he said. He looked like he was speaking to a ghost.

"Of course I was coming, Ted. You didn't think I'd miss seeing my star pupil getting his award, did you?"

I reached for the medal he was holding, which was attached to a blue ribbon. He dropped it into my hand.

"Let's see what you got," I said. He looked at me like I'd just asked him to jump off a cliff. His mind was off somewhere in outer space. On one side of the medal were the words

1957 Junior Achievement Award, Science

First Place

On the other side were two hands holding up a torch, and above that an atom.

"What did you do, anyway?" I asked him.

"Do?" he asked.

"Yeah, do, you know, to get this award?"

He still couldn't think, so Miss Jeannie said it for him, "Ted conducted important research in plasma physics."

"Plasma physics, huh." I said. "What's that?" I asked her. If I'd asked Ted what two plus two was, I honestly don't think he could have come up with the answer. His eyes were empty, as if his brain had been sucked from his skull.

"It's complicated stuff," Miss Jeannie said. "It's way beyond me."

The old man handed Miss Jeannie a glass of soda. I looked into his eyes when he did it, but I didn't see anything there. I'd have to fix that.

"Thank you, Mr. McTavish," she said.

"Henry," he said.

"Henry, then," she said. Her smile was killing me. The old man looked away, and turned to Ted.

"I'm proud of you Ted. I want you to take your gift as far as it can take you. Don't let anything hold you back."

"It's wonderful that Princeton is so close, Henry, isn't it? Ted needn't go anywhere to extend his studies, Miss Jeannie said."

She smiled at the old man, and then at Ted. Ted looked at her and tried to smile, but it didn't take. He was sweating like a pig, I suddenly noticed. Then it hit me. Mr. Genius was flustered as hell. Her beauty was way too much for him. He was such a putz with the opposite sex it made me sick. Man, if I was her age, I'd be all over her. But it was okay I wasn't; my time would come with women. Not with Miss Jeannie, of course, who would be an old bag by the time I got to be her age.

"Congratulations, Ted," we heard this guy say. He came up to Ted and put a hand on his shoulder.

"Thank you, sir," Ted said.

The guy offered his hand to the old man. "Bob Peterson, Chairman of the nominating committee."

"Henry McTavish," the old man said.

"Missus McTavish, I presume," he said to Miss Jeannie.

"No, I'm Ted's science teacher from his junior yeahr, Jeannie Sullivan."

"Oh, I see," Peterson said. "You both must be very proud. Heck, we're all proud of what Ted's accomplished, it's remarkable for a man of his young age. I hear Princeton is in the cards," he said to Ted.

"Yes sir, hopefully sir," Ted squeaked.

"Oh, I'm sure they'll be glad to have you," Peterson said, and made a phony laugh. He looked at me. The guy had on a flannel jacket, and it smelled like it had just come out of a musty closet for the first time in forever. Long hairs were shooting out from his ears, and his glasses made his eyes look beady. He looked fishy to me, like he was one of those phony politician types. I had to look nearly straight up to look into that face of his. The guy was way over six feet. "So, son, what do you think of your brother?" he asked me.

I don't know why I said it, other than that I can be a real jerk sometimes, especially when I'm around a real jerk like this Peterson toad. If I'd been thinking, I wouldn't have said what I did, since Miss Jeannie was standing right next to me. I needed her to get to like us, and not think of me, the future step kid I hoped to be, as a wise guy. But as it turned out, she was cool.

"I think it's too bad he picked something like plasma physics to do his project on."

"Oh, why's that?" Peterson asked.

I looked at Ted. He made a dark look. He wanted to sock me one already. "I think he should have done it on satellites instead. I hear we're going to launch one soon."

"Well," Peterson said. "Why don't *you* start working on that? Maybe you'll win an award with it. What do you think, Ted? Sounds like your brother here is on to something."

"He already did a project on satellites. I think he's just kidding to be funny," Ted said.

"Oh, ha, for a science fair, did you?" Peterson asked me. He then made a slurping sound in his glass as he took a sip of his soda. The ice was noisy when he tipped the glass back down. I wasn't liking this guy.

"Yup, for a science fair," I told him.

"Well, did you win?"

"Nah, I was disqualified," I said.

"Oh, that's too bad," Peterson said. He tightened his grip on Ted's shoulder and changed the subject. "Well Ted, continued good luck, and-"

"You want to know why I was disqualified?" I cut him off.

"Danny," the old man said. "I don't think Mr. Peterson needs to know why your project was disqualified."

"It's because I trusted these two guys from Princeton who helped me with the project, and they screwed up."

Miss Jeannie laughed. I looked at her and fell in love all over again. I laughed too.

"You don't say?" she asked. "How did that happen?"

"They didn't screw up," Ted interrupted. "I really don't see what this has to do with anything."

Ted was getting steamed. And I was making Miss Jeannie laugh. It was the best of both worlds.

"Oh, c'mon Ted, let's hear it Danny," she said.

"Well, I had read about what Mr. Clarke said about putting satellites in geosynchronous orbit and all, so I designed my project to have a bunch of satellites suspended above and around the earth, with stations beaming signals up to the satellites and back down again. We used synchronous lighting."

"That's very impressive, Danny," Miss Jeannie said. "Ted, you never mentioned you had such a clever brother."

Ted opened his mouth, but nothing came out. He looked at me and smoldered.

"So what about the Princeton boys, Danny?" she asked. "What did they do wrong."

"Well, I had them construct for me, on account of a deal I worked out, the whole thing, and they put a label on one of the steel balls that said earth. Only it came loose during the exhibiting night, and underneath it, it said property of Princeton. So my teacher and the rest of the judges disqualified me."

"Who was your teacher?" she asked.

"Mr. Jacobs," I told her.

"Oh, how silly," she said. "Don't you think that's a shame, Ted, what they did to your brother?"

"Well, I'd best be going," Peterson piped up, and nodded.

We told him goodbye, and the big lout stomped off.

"I'd best be going also," Miss Jeannie said. "It was nice seeing you again, Henry, and nice meeting you, Danny."

"Likewise," I said. Little could she have imagined that I was determined to make her a big part of our family.

"Goodnight Ted. I'll see around in school in the fall," she said.

Ted only nodded his head.

"Goodnight, Jeannie," the old man said. "And thanks for coming."

"Bye bye," she said, and disappeared into the crowd. I missed her already.

Well boys, let's head for home," the old man said, and sighed.

"She's a real nice lady, isn't she dad," I said.

The old man put a hand on my shoulder, "Very nice, yes," he said.

19

Of course, Ted wanted to beat the crap out of me. He was really hot when we got home. When we got upstairs to our room, he closed the door.

"Ok, buster," he said, "you've really done it this time." He leaped at me. We went sprawling onto my bed, me on my back and he straddled on top. He started beating me, but at the same time he was desperately trying to turn me over to get at my face. He couldn't do it, so then he began to hammer at the back of my head.

"What did I do?" I managed to say into my pillow.

"You embarrassed the hell out of me in front of two important people, Mr. Peterson and Miss Sullivan. You're always sticking your crummy life into mine. First you stuck your nose into my life at Princeton, and now this." He kept on beating the hell out of me, but it didn't hurt too badly. But if I didn't get him off of me, I supposed I'd eventually be beaten to a pulp.

"Okay, okay, cut it out, I'm sorry," I told him. "Really, I am. You can have your life to yourself, I'll leave it alone. I won't go near anyone you know. Now get off."

"You're such a swine," he said.

"I didn't think it was such a big deal. Nobody cares about what I said. What you did is terrific."

"It doesn't matter what you think, you always screw up my life," he said.

He kept trying to turn me over, but gave up and swiped the side of my face with a right.

"Lighten up, will ya?" I said. "When was the last time you laughed about anything?"

That stopped him. "What are you talking about?" he asked.

"Well, what'ya mean, what do I mean. You know what I'm saying. When was the last time you thought anything was funny?"

"I don't know, Danny." He got off. He started for the bathroom.

"Ted."

"What."

"Wait a minute."

"What."

"All that research, does it make you happy?"

"It's very satisfying. So I suppose it makes me happy, then."

"Ok, good, but it doesn't make you laugh."

"No, my studies do not make me laugh, you're right."

"So, when was the last time you had a good laugh? I'll bet if you think about it, it was with me. Something silly we did together, like that time we got chased by that guy when we dug a hole in his garden 'cause we thought there was buried treasure in it, remember? Or when we went to Seaside Heights, and went to that funhouse. You're growing up too fast, man. Look at me. I'm an idiot, but I have fun. I guess it's because I'm an idiot, like my friends."

"I've told you before Danny, you're not an idiot. You insult your family when you act like one. You're smart,

I can see it. You get good grades when you want to. You just
don't give a shit. But you know what?" he asked.

"What?"

He turned around to face me. "You're the kind of
guy who becomes successful. You're good with people.
They listen to what you have to say, even if what you say is
ridiculous."

"Mom once told me I should be a comedian when I
grow up. She said I make people laugh.

"Well, you don't make me laugh."

"You need to get some new friends. Ones that can
make you laugh."

"You know that guy Steve you met at Princeton, the
ham radio guy?" he asked.

"Yeah, what about him?"

"He's funny, he makes me laugh. So there."

On the radio, or in person?"

"Both, why?"

"Just askin'" I said.

He went into our bathroom and closed the door.

I got into my pajamas and laid back down, and put
my arms behind my head on the pillow. I looked at the back
of our bedroom door. There was my picture in the center of
all the Yankees, pitching in Little League. If I made it to the
bigs someday, the old lady wouldn't see it, at least from
down here. It was shaping up to be an interesting summer,
after all. There was six weeks left until school. The pennant
race was heating up, and I'd try to make it to the Stadium.
And another race would begin, a race to get Miss Jeannie
and the old man together before I had to go back to school.

That next morning, I decided I had to make a plan of action. The first thing I had to do was to find out where Jeannie Sullivan lived. I looked her name up in the phone book. There were eight Jean Sullivans and one J. Sullivan. I was able to eliminate five of them after looking at a map, figuring they lived too far away from the high school.

I ripped out the part of the page I needed, drew a map, and called up the guys. I told them to meet me down at the ball field.

"Ok, what now Danny boy?" Jerry asked. "What'ya got for us?"

"We've got a mission," I said.

"Uh huh," Lance said. "What kind of trouble are we gonna get in this time?" Lance asked.

"No trouble," I said. "But it has to do with a broad, though."

"Why am I not surprised?" Lance said. "And you're just a kid. What's going to happen when you become an adult? You gonna have forty girl friends and forty wives?"

"Ha ha," I said. "This is serious business." I held up the piece of paper from the phone book. "These are the names of four Jeannie or J Sullivans. One of them is the one I am looking for. We have to find where the right one lives. I need your guys help."

Lance looked at Jerry. "Can you believe this guy?" Jerry shrugged.

"This a treasure hunt or something?" Lance asked. "So whose the real Jeannie Sullivan, and how come you gotta find out where she lives?"

"I met her last night. She was Ted's science teacher last yeahr. She sat next to me at the awards ceremony."

"So?" Lance asked.

"So, I've got to have her get hitched to the old man,"

"What!" Lance yelled.

"Oh man, Danny, this is your best scheme yet," Jerry said, and beamed.

"Look, don't ask me why. You'll know when you see her. You guys have to meet these Sullivan people; I can't do it. You know, knock on their door, and then after I see if it's her, you just say, "Oh, sorry, I got the wrong Jean Sullivan.""

"Where you gonna be?" Lance asked.

"Hiding, but so I can see if it's her."

"You're crazy," Lance said. "Let me guess, she's hot, right? So now you want her to be your new old lady."

"I wouldn't put it that way," I said. But he was sort of right.

I fished out from my pocket the map and unfolded it. "And look, I even made a map of the locations of the addresses. I figured we'd start with the closest to the school, and work our way around. Even if it takes the last one to find her, I figure we'll go ten miles, tops."

"Ten miles!" Lance cried.

"That ain't far," I said.

"On a racetrack, maybe," he said. "But around here? That'll take all day."

I looked at my Timex. It said ten o'clock. "We start now, we'll be done by two at the latest. And that's with stopping to eat."

"Eat?" Jerry asked.

"Yeah, I figure on the way to stop three, if we haven't found her yet, we'd stop by the bowling alley, and get some grub."

"So what's she like, Danny?" Jerry asked.

"You'll see," I said.

"She really was Ted's teacher, like you said?" he asked.

"Yeah, sure," I said. "Why not?"

"What if she doesn't want to marry your old man? I mean, how you gonna get them together and all that?"

"It's stupid, the stupidest idea he's ever had," Lance said.

"The trick is," I said, "is to get them together, but make it seem like an accident."

"How you going to do that?" Jerry asked.

I shrugged. "I haven't gotten that far, yet. First things first. You guys ready?"

Lance sighed and picked up his bike. "We've done a lot of screwy thing together, but this one takes the cake," he said.

"I tell you what," I said. "We'll stop at old Greenburg's and get a pack of cards, too."

"Yeah, yeah, let's just go," Lance said.

We hit the road, and the first place took about thirty minutes to get to.

"Hey, I know this place," Lance said. "Ain't no way your school teacher lives out this way. Not unless she lives with rich parents. All these places out here are expensive."

We found the street, and then the number.

"Nice pad," Jerry whistled. "No way she lives here, Danny."

"No place to hide either," I said. "Yeah, this can't be it."

"Ok, what's next?" Lance asked.

I took out the map. "It's about four miles from here."

"Let me see that," Lance said. "You sure this is the way?" he asked.

"Yeah, look, I drew it all out."

"We gotta take the highway, we go that way," Lance said.

"So?" I asked.

"So that's too dangerous," he said.

"It's the shortest way," I told him.

"May be," Lance said, "but my old lady takes Julie out that way for her piano lessons, and I don't feel like getting run down by some humungous truck the size of Montana. You won't see trucks like that you go my way."

"Ok, whatever you say," I agreed. "You lead the way."

We had to stop three times to rest before we got to the next address. The road dipped and rose too many times, and it was hot as hell. At the third stop, we pulled our bikes off where we saw an abandoned silo. We walked our bikes in through waist high grass and leaned them up against the side of it.

"Let's go in," Jerry said.

We went through an open doorway. Against the outer wall was an old rusty pitchfork, and on some shelves was a pair of stiff, crusty looking gloves. I stepped through another opening into the center and looked up. "Hey anybody up there?" I yelled. My voice rang like a bell.

"Miss Sullivan, darling, you there in the hayloft?" Jerry hollered.

"Barns have haylofts, you idiot," I said. "Do you see a hayloft?"

Jerry made kissing sounds. I shoved him. "Don't go making fun of my future step mom, now."

"She ain't gonna be your mom," Jerry said. "How old is she, anyway?"

"Thirty-two, maybe."

"How do you know she ain't married?"

"On account of she didn't have a wedding ring, or one of those engagement rings either. She ain't married."

"If she's so hot, how come she ain't been married yet?" Jerry asked.

"I didn't say she was hot, she's nice, is all."

"Yeah, yeah," Lance said. "She ain't hot like this place is air conditioned."

"She's not going to want to marry your old man, no way," Jerry said. "She'll want kids of her own, not you two guys. And your old man's too old to want to have kids again. Plus, he might not have a job pretty soon. All those things ad up."

I hated to think it, but he was right. I was fooling myself. It depressed the hell out of me. "I've got to try," I said.

"Why don't you invite her to the bowling alley?" Jerry asked.

"Nah, that's no good. The old man's always behind the bar, and all those stinking losers are always around."

"But where else she gonna see him? He's always there," Jerry said.

"You're making this difficult, already. Let's just find out where she lives, first," I said.

We went back outside, and saw a horse and rider a couple hundred yards off.

"Hey, maybe it's your tittie girl, Danny, what's her name?" Jerry said.

"Yeah, right. Old Molly and her titties are in California. And she can have her goddamn titties or give them to someone else to look at. Even if she lived here, I'd never want to see her again."

"You didn't like her showing everybody her titties, huh?" Jerry asked.

"She just seemed an all around jerk. Maybe it's because she's only twelve. I guess I should have expected she'd act that way."

"I don't know of any other girl showing her titties around like she does, let alone a twelve yeahr old girl," Lance said.

"Yeah, but you don't know any girls with titties like that, period," Jerry said.

"So you saying any girl with tits like Molly's gonna show them around?" Lance asked.

"Maybe if she's twelve," I cut in. "I'll bet when she grows up a bit, she'll stop doing that. I'd say a chest like she's got is unprecedented on a twelve yeahr old."

"I like that, unprecedented," Jerry said.

"I'll bet this hunt we're on is unprecedented," Lance said. "I mean, who ever heard of a fourteen yeahr old kid trying to find out where some broad lives he met the night before, so he can convince her and his old man to get hitched. That's a new one."

"How would you know?" I asked him. "I remember my grandfather once saying that chances are if you think of something, like an invention, that you think no one else has ever thought of or done before, no matter what it is, no matter how crazy, some guys already done it. So I bet some kids done what I'm doing."

"That's nuts," Lance said. "Your grandfather's saying that it ain't ever worth trying to come up with something original?"

"I think a lot of times," I said, "people come up with new stuff, and they just don't know what to do with it. Some time later, another guy picks up the idea, and runs with it. Or maybe, the world's not ready for an idea, until later."

"What the hell we talkin' about, anyway?" Lance asked. "Lets go. What time is it?"

"Almost twelve," I said.

"Holy shit!" Lance said. "We blew two hours and we're not even at our second destination."

"Well hell," I said, "this way you got us goin' on ain't exactly a short cut, remember?"

"We'll be there soon," Lance said.

We came to the joint about twenty minutes later. It was a tiny row house. The only place I could hide behind was a fire hydrant, which wasn't too good, but would have to do.

"Ok guys, go knock on the door," I said.

"This is stupid," Lance said.

"You should have said that two hours ago," I said.

"I did, remember?"

"I'll do it," Jerry said. "But what if she's not home?"

He had a point. "Just try."

Lance went with him. Jerry pushed the doorbell, and I could hear it ring from behind the hydrant. No one came to the door, so they rang it again.

"What's you doin?" a voice asked and I jumped. Behind me was this little girl, maybe four.

"Christ, kid, you scared the bejeesus out of me. Go away," I told her and waved her away.

"What's those two guys doin?" she asked and pointed. "They-"

"Shhhh!" I said. "Go away!" I heard the door open.

"They friends of yours?" she asked.

"Yeah, now go away," I said.

I heard voices, but I couldn't get a peek because the girl was standing next to me and then I heard a woman's voice say,

"Nancy, you get over here, right now!"

"But there's a boy hiding right here behind the fire hydrant," she yelled and pointed at me.

"Get away then," the broad said, "and come inside." I heard footsteps on the porch, and then on the front walk. I stood up.

"May I ask what you're doing, young man?" she asked.

"Oh, sorry, we thought you were someone else, a different Jeannie Sullivan. I was going to surprise her."

"Did he hurt you darling?" she said to her little snot.

"Uhuh," the snot said. "What was he doing behind that fire hydrant, making a surprise, mommy?"

"Come on boys," I said.

This is great," Lance said when he came alongside.

"Let's eat, I'm starved," I said.

Along the way to the lanes, we stopped at Greenburg's.

"Pack of baseball cards," I told old man Greenburg, who sat behind the counter.

He plopped it down, and I plopped down my dime. I unwrapped it, and broke the sheet of gum into thirds, and handed the boys a piece. I shoved one into my mouth. It tasted like gum and cardboard, like always. I flipped the stack.

"Bobby Richardson," I said. "I got three, how 'bout you guys."

"Got 'em," Jerry said.

"Me too," Lance said.

"You're smackin' your gum in my eardrum, for Pete's sake," I told Lance.

"Willie Mays," Lance chomped, "we don't like him."

"Yeah, but I'm keepin' all I can get of his," I said. "Might be worth something someday. Who the hell's this guy?" I asked. The next card was a guy on the Pirates I'd never heard of.

There weren't any more Yankees in the pack. "Hey, Mr. Greenburg," Lance said, "How come we don't get just Yankee cards? Is that so we keep buying packs?"

"Look, kid," Greenburg said, "the card company ain't goin' to sort the cards for you. It don't matter if you live in Jersey or Pittsburgh, they don't care."

"Yeah, ok," Lance said.

"Hey Danny," Jerry said, "you ever tell Mr. Greenburg about the collection you got from old man Sweet?"

"Nope," I said.

"He gave you his collection, son?"

"No, his wife did," I told him.

"You got some great stuff then, hold onto it," Greenburg said.

"Well, he gave away the Johnny Mize signed uniform," Jerry said, "but he got it back. But he didn't get back, what was that card that Professor guy kept?"

"It doesn't matter," I said. "I got some crap is all. C'mon fellas."

We made our way to the lanes, but not before we each stuck a card into the spokes of our front wheels. They flapped when we rode.

"You should have put that Mays card in there, Danny," Jerry said.

"Like I said, they might be worth holding onto," I said.

"He's good, but not as good as Mickey," Lance said.

"Nobody's as good as Mickey," Jerry said. "He's gonna break Ruth's sixty home run record some day, you'll see."

"If anybody'll do it, the Mick will," I said.

"When we got to the lanes, I told the guys, "Now don't go saying anything to the old man or anyone else about what we're up to." We took seats at the bar. I looked out at the lanes. Three were busy. Sniffy and a buddy of his were working them.

"What are you boys up to?" the old man asked. He shoved three sodas our way.

"Just ridin'" I said. "Any hot dogs on?"

"A pit stop, huh?" the old man asked. He seemed a bit cheerful. It was the first time I'd seen a hint of it since the old lady left us.

He went over to the boiler and picked out three dogs, stuffed them into buns, and put them on plates. He then took the top off the can of potato chips, tossed a handful on each plate, and brought us the chow.

"Thanks loads, Mr. McTavish," Lance said.

"Yeah, thank Mr. McTavish," Jerry said.

"Thanks, pops," I said. "You need us tonight, right?" I asked.

"Yeah, sure," he said. "You boys gonna work?"

"Sure," we all mumbled between chews.

"Say dad, you ever think of taking a night off?" I asked.

"I do, sometimes, you know that. Why?"

"But you never know when?"

"Sure I do, I have to arrange with Mr. Conrad to take over for me. Your mother and I would go out once in a while, while he watched the place."

I nodded. "I was just curious about it."

We finished and started to leave. "See you at home, son," the old man said. "Seven o'clock, right boys?"

"See ya then, Mr. McTavish. Thanks again," the boys said.

We got outside. "Two to go, maybe," I said.

I got out the map. "It's not far. Three miles, maybe."

We took off, and when we got about halfway there, Jerry said he had to take a crap something awful.

"There's no place for you to go," I told him.

"I can go off to the side somewhere," he said.

"Where?" I asked him. "There's no place to hide. There's gotta be places near the next stop, maybe just before it. We'll be there in ten minutes if we push it."

"Somethins' pushin' out of me," Jerry winced.

He groaned the rest of the way, and then we came to the place.

"Damn, it's an apartment building," I said. "You guys go inside the front door, and see if they're names on mailboxes."

They went in, and came out soon after. "She's in apartment two k," Lance said.

"Ok, listen, you guys knock on her door, and if she comes out, just say you're looking for Jeannie Sullivan. I'll be downstairs listening. She'll say she's Sullivan, and ask what' it's about."

"So what do we say then?" Lance asked.

"Ask her if she's the lady who ordered a refrigerator. That you've got one to deliver."

"Us?" Lance asked. "Wouldn't she think adults would deliver a stinking refrigerator?"

"Say you're the bosses' kid. Just get her talking. I'll be able to tell if it's her."

"Well, hell Danny, just tell us what she looks like," Lance said. "You said she's about thirty. What color hair she got?"

"Brown, and kinda curly. She's got brown eyes too, I'm pretty sure. And she's pretty and smells nice."

"What kind of description is that? Let's go Jerry."

They stomped up two landings while I hid under the stairwell. I heard them knock. It sounded loud. A few moments later, I heard the door squeak open. Then I heard Jeannie's voice.

"Yes?" she asked.

"Ah, yes," I heard Lance say. "Uh, we're here to deliver a refrigerator?"

"Ma'am," I heard Jerry say. "You got a bathroom? I gotta go somethin' awful."

"Who sent you boys, really?" Jeannie asked.

There was no reply, and then a few seconds later came a racket as the boys beat it down the stairs. I came out of hiding just in time to get run over on their way out the door. I hightailed it out behind them, and ran across the front yard, hoping like hell she didn't have a view out that way. We jumped on our bikes and pumped for all we were worth. Jerry spied a gas station and ditched his bike at full speed and ran into the bathroom on the side of the place.

"That was real smooth," I said to Lance.

"Could you tell if it was her?" Lance asked me.

"Yeah, it was Jeannie."

"Man, she's gorgeous all right."

"How could you tell, you hardly saw her."

"I saw her long enough to know," Lance said.

20

I sent the ball back and jumped up on the shelf.

"So what now, Danny? Jerry asked from his lane. "You know where she lives, so what's the plan?"

"Well, I started one," I said

"Yeah, what?" Jerry asked.

"When I got home, I took a piece of paper and drew a line down the middle. On the left side I wrote positives and on the right, negatives."

"What's that mean?" Jerry asked.

I left the shelf and cleared pins. "Of the old man and his situation, you know good points and bad points, things he's got going for him, and things that aren't so hot, from a dame perspective."

"What for?" Jerry asked.

"Look, Miss Jeannie's got a lot going for her. She's beautiful, she's sweet, and she's pretty smart seeing as she's a science teacher and all. You told me she's not going to want to get mixed up with a guy like my old man whose already got two kids, and going to lose his business. I have to focus on the good and somehow fix the bad."

"How you gonna do that?" he asked. "What'd you write?"

"I got the paper in my pocket," I said.

"You got it with you? What for?"

"I figured if I looked at it, I could come up with ideas about it."

"Let me see it," Jerry said.

"You can't, we're too damn busy," I told him.

"Well, how you gonna read it, then?" he said.

"I didn't think we'd be so busy." My Timex said near eight thirty, and the lanes were hopping. But by nine, things slowed down, so only two lanes were working, Lance and Sniffy's.

"Let's have a look," Lance said.

We sat on the shelf behind lane one, and I took out the paper. On it I had written:

POSITIVES	NEGATIVES
About same age as Jeannie	-a little older.
Ted can be a real pain in the ass	
Not bad looking guy	I can be a pain in the ass
Fun?	Will lose business pretty soon
Owns bowling alley	Doesn't have much time off
Has genius kid	
Has me	
Romantic	
Needs a woman for cooking, cleaning,	
And you know what, etc.	
Pretty smart	
Works hard	
Can cook some	
Jeannie his type	
Jeannie already knows Ted	

"I don't think it's gonna happen," Jerry said.

"Yeah, you already said that," I told him.

"Yeah, but look, you got you and Ted on the positives, but I'm tellin' ya, they're negatives only. A lady that age doesn't want to marry a guy with two kids like you guys. And why should she give a crap Ted's a genius?"

"You kidding?" She's his science teacher, remember? She's so proud of him, she said. She'd probably go bonkers to have a kid like him. So if she married the old man, she'd have an instant genius kid. If he becomes famous, then she'd be known as his old lady. She'd think that was cool."

"That's crazy," Jerry said. "And you got you on the positive side. Ain't nothing positive about you. I mean, you're a good buddy, and you can be funny, and all, but you'd be no good reason for her to want to marry your old man. You even got both of you on the negative, how can you be on both sides?"

"I'm just trying to put down the positives and the negatives, as I see it."

"You should just stick to your old man. Or it gets messy."

"Yeah, maybe.

"He's a little older than she is, you figure, that's good. He ain't bad looking?"

"We both squinted to get a look at the old man who was behind the bar, as if we couldn't remember what he looked like.

"Yeah, I suppose," Jerry agreed. "But we're guys. Who knows what Jeannie thinks? Besides, how do you know she doesn't have a boy friend?"

I hadn't really thought about that, but if she did, I just would consider that to be another hurdle. "I don't. But I guess I could spend some time snoopin' around to find out."

"If she does, what are you gonna do then?" Jerry asked.

I shrugged. "I'll cross that bridge if there is one," I said.

"He's fun?" Jerry read.

"Yeah, why not? He's as much fun as the next guy, I guess."

"Your old man's no fun 'cause he ain't got no time to have fun. You say right here he's a hard worker. Well, that all he ever seems to do."

"Nah, that's not true," I said.

"Well, is he funny?" Jerry asked.

I thought about it. "Not really. I mean, he'll crack a joke once in a while, kid around a bit, stuff like that."

"Well, he doesn't sound like too much fun to me," Jerry said. "And you got here he's got a bowling alley. But not for long."

"Well, I wrote it down because it shows he's enterprising," I said.

"You got here he's romantic? How would you know?"

"Well, I mean, he and the old lady would go out, just the two of them, once in a while. And, we could hear them laughing sometimes when they got home." I remembered those sometimes, and suddenly felt shitty.

"What's this?" Jerry asked. "You got here, 'he needs someone to cook and clean, and you know what?'"

"Hey, the old man's still a young guy. He's, you know, he needs a woman, or he's gonna sometime."

"Yeah," Jerry agreed. He put a hand on my arm. "Look Jerry."

The old man was leaning over the bar, and opposite him was a broad I'd never seen before. She was holding a drink in one hand, and a cigarette in another, and it seemed they were yakking it up pretty friendly like. She gave a laugh, and then he laughed. She was all dolled up, too dolled up to suit me. Her hair was tied up in a thick bun. She took a drag on her cigarette, then turned to one side and blew.

"Who's that dame?" Jerry asked. "You ever seen her before?"

"No," I said.

"You know Danny, word gets around about a guy, you know what I'm trying to say."

"Yeah, I know, but the old man would never be interested in a dame like that. Let's see what they're talkin' about."

I started to go, but Jerry grabbed me again.

"You can't do that!" Jerry said. "You don't think they'll see you up there, spyin' on them? Do ya think they'll just keep talkin' about the same stuff?"

"Hey, they ain't talkin' about nuthin', that's my old man, remember. They're probably just talking about what's on the television." I didn't believe that, but I just had to check this dame out close.

We walked along the wall next to lane one, and I noticed the guy on Lance's lane finish up. Lance started to follow us.

I took a seat three down from the broad at the bar, and the boys took the next two away. The old man and she were still gabbin' away like there was no tomorrow.

I heard the old man, say, "Yeah, I know what you mean, Tracy."

"You ought to come on over some time, Henry, you'll have a lot of fun."

"You hear that?" Jerry whispered in my ear.

"Shut up," I whispered back. I kept my gaze on the television.

"Well, we'll see," the old man was saying. I felt him look over at me, and he came over.

"Well boys, another day. Thanks for working," he said.

"Yeah, sure," we all said.

"You boys thirsty?" he asked.

"Yeah, sure," we all answered. The dame was staring me down, and the old man had a stupid look on his face.

He slid us our soda. "Guess we'd better start to clean up," I said to the guys.

Then the dame asked, "Henry, this one of your boys?"

"Oh, yeah," he told her.

She blew smoke out of the side of her mouth as she faced me. "Hey there, sport," she said. "Hey Henry, if this guy's your younger, he looks old enough to watch himself if you come over."

"Oh, it's not that," he said, "Ted's around anyway, it's just that I haven't done that sort of thing in a long time."

"What the matter," the dame asked, "you afraid of playing with a dame?"

Man, she sure didn't care that I was in hearing range. She was after the old man, for sure. And I was damned if he'd start fooling around with a cheap looking floozy like her. Plus my old man would never go out with a broad who smoked.

Behind me I heard, "You ready Tracy?"

She stubbed out her cigarette and got up. The big lout who had been bowling on Lance's lane put a hand around her shoulder.

"I was just tellin' Henry he oughta come around Wednesday for cards. I think he's too chicken to lose to a dame, is his problem," she said.

"Nah," the old man said. "I'm just not much for gambling. I always lose, ha ha."

"See, I told ya," the lout said. He looked at me. "This your kid?"

"Yeah," the old man said. "This is my younger one, Danny, Danny this is George."

"Hi," I said.

He put a sweaty hand out. He took mine and nearly crushed it.

"Danny's a hard worker, George," the old man said. "I don't know what I'd do without him."

"See ya next time, boys," George said, and he and Tracy left.

"That was close," Jerry whispered.

"Close nuthin'," I said. "We were just imagining things, is all."

When we got home, I lay in bed thinking about that dame, Tracy, and wondered whether the old man could ever be attracted to a broad like that. I didn't think so, but you never knew, especially if the wrong dame like that came on hard to him. I knew how it was, and I was only fourteen. He didn't have time for women, to take the time to pick the right one, anyway. I'm sure he wasn't ready for one; that time would come. He didn't need to meet some stranger, not when Miss Jeannie was around.

21

"See ya later, son."

"What do you mean, dad? Where are you going?"

"Out, on a date."

"A date? Who's watching the lanes?"

"Mr. Conrad. Better get out, I'm running late."

"You seeing someone?"

"Not unless you get out of the car."

"Yeah, ok. How am I getting home?"

"If I'm not back by the time we close, Mr. Conrad will give you a ride."

"Can I ask who your date's with?"

"No, son. Now get along."

"Sure, have a good time." I barely got the door closed in time before he floored it.

I went inside the lanes. The place was quiet, except for the television. No one was bowling, and the lanes were dark. I looked at the back shelf, and no pin boys were there. The bar was full. I noticed the television was turned to the Ernie Kovacs show.

Mr. Conrad was behind the bar. I went to its side entrance and asked him, *"Mr. Conrad, that's not supposed to be on yet."* He didn't hear me. He was too busy talking it up with some broad.

"Hey, Mr. Conrad, how come the Ernie Kovacs show is on? Turn it off."

He still didn't pay any attention to me. And then I realized everyone at the bar was a dame, dolled up and all, drinking and smoking away. I was angry as hell.

I told the dame at the bar, "Excuse me," and then said, "Mr. Conrad, where are all the pin boys? How come no one's bowling?"

"This Henry's kid?" the floozy asked.

"Yeah, pain in the ass, ain't he?" Mr. Conrad said. "Kid doesn't know his place."

"What are you talking about?" I yelled. "How come no one's bowling?"

"Get lost, kid," he said. "You know the joint closed down six months ago. We're just a bar now."

I heard a noise behind me, and I turned to look. A lady was sweeping the floor, her back was to me. She looked somehow familiar, but she was dressed in rags. I felt badly for her. I walked over to her, but when I came close, she turned away, so I couldn't see her face.

"Hi," I said. She didn't answer. "Hi, need some help?" I asked.

She shook her head.

I went back to the bar. "Mr. Conrad, can you tell me who that woman is sweeping up the floor?"

"What's the matter with you, boy?" he asked. "Can't you tell your old lady when you see her?"

"How can you say that?" I yelled. "You know that can't be her!"

I ran back to her, and tried to turn her around, but she kept turning the other way, so I never saw her face.

"Ma? Ma, that you?" I asked, but I knew that was impossible.

*The woman lowered her head and stopped sweeping.
Go away, son," she said. Her voice sounded familiar, but I
wasn't sure.*

"Ma, that really you?"

*"You'd better leave, Danny, before he comes back
and picks up another one."*

*"Who, what are you talking about? Mom, mom, is
that you?"*

*I heard the door open. I turned to look, and in came
the old man behind Tracy. They went to the bar, and the old
man slapped Tracy on the rear.*

*"Not bad, kiddo," he told her. "Who wants to be
next?"*

*A dame hopped up from the bar, and threw her arms
around the old man. Tracy took her place on the stool.*

"Dad, what's happening?" I cried.

*He turned to me and said, "Nothin' to be concerned
about, son. You go home with Mr. Conrad like I told you, if
I'm late."*

*"Dad, who is that lady?" I asked, pointing to the
floor sweeper. She had her back to us, standing still with her
head down.*

*"She'll be ok, don't you worry about it," he
answered. "Somebody's gotta earn their keep around here."*

*The dame hanging all over the old man giggled, and
they moved towards the door. The old man was having a
tough time of it; the dame was a dead weight, her feet
dragging along the floor.*

"Dad, dad!" I hollered, but he ignored me and left.

*I screamed to Tracy, "What happened, tell me what
happened? What's this all about?"*

"Your old man's quite the romantic, like you wrote, Danny boy." She blew smoke in my face. *"And he sure ain't bad looking to boot! I told 'em he comes with too much baggage, though, you know, you two guys, so I had him ditch me back here."*

I turned, and the floor sweeper was gone.

22

"You're right, Jerry, we've got to find out if she's got a boyfriend," I said.

"You said that Jerry?" Lance asked. "What did ya do that for? Now we have to go on a wild goose chase to find out about a boyfriend?"

"What wild goose chase?" I said. "If she's got a boyfriend, he'll come to her place, won't he?"

"So what are we supposed to do, hang out at her place at all hours of the night, and see if some guy picks her up?"

We were at the ball field, trying to figure out the next step.

"So what if we find out she's got one?" Jerry asked. "We gonna shoot him?"

"Maybe we can make things difficult for him," I said. "You know, monkey around with his car. Call her up and pretend to be him and say mean things."

"That's stupid," Lance said.

"Well, I have to find out," I said. "I have to know what I'm up against, don't I? And I have to have your guys help."

"You're going to far this time, Danny," Lance said. "What do you need our help for anyway?"

"On account of she knows me. She doesn't know you guys."

"Yeah, she does," Lance said. "She saw us, yesterday, remember?"

"Yeah, but she doesn't know who you guys are. If she sees you guys again, maybe she'll just think it's a coincidence."

"Danny," Jerry said, "why can't you just go to her place and talk to her?"

"Look at it this way," I said. "Let's say she's got a boyfriend, and funny things start to happen to him, and she knows I've been hangin' around, and then I get her fixed up with my old man, how would that look?"

"I don't get it, how would that look?" Lance asked.

"I mean, she'd maybe get suspicious I had something to do with it, she splitting up with her boyfriend, I mean."

"He's got a point," Jerry said.

"Nah, she's not gonna think you had anything to do with her stinking boyfriend, you're just stalling," Lance said.

"What'ya mean?" I asked.

"You just haven't figured out how you're going to get your old man and she together," Lance said.

"Your just chicken to find out if she's got a boyfriend," I said.

"What'ya mean?" Lance asked.

"Your afraid if we mess things up for him with Miss Jeannie, he'll find out you had something to do with it, and he'll come after you."

"Yeah? Well why should I help you then, if I'm so afraid? Why should Jerry and I help with a stupid idea that's not going to work anyway?" Lance said.

I never said you had to," I said. "I can't make you help. It's just important to me, so I figured you guys would want to help."

"Well, I'll help, but I'm not chicken," Lance said.

"Okay," I said. "I still say I need to find out whether she's got a boyfriend. Jerry's the one who thought about that, I didn't."

"So what do we do?" Jerry asked. "We can't keep riding our bikes over to her place until we find out if she's got one. It's too far. And how we gonna know she doesn't have one, if she doesn't have one?"

"I tell you what," I said. "I'll wait until Saturday night. I'll ask the old man in the mean time whether I can take the night off. If she's got a boyfriend, she'll be seeing him then.

"Where you going to hangout?" Jerry asked.

"Weren't there trees across the street? I can hide behind them."

"Suit yourself," Lance said.

"I'll go with you," Jerry said.

"You sure?" I asked.

"Yeah, why not? I've got two sleeping bags. Why don't you tell your old man that you're sleeping over at my place, and we'll ride from there."

"Sounds good," I said. "This time we'll go direct to her place. I bet we can be there in an hour if we push it. I'll be over about five-thirty."

"Ok, see you then," Jerry said.

When I got home, I asked the old man if I could take Saturday night off to be with the guys.

"Saturday?" he asked. "Why Saturday, Danny? You know that's our busiest night."

"Yeah, but Lance is having a party," I told him. "So the other guys aren't coming. Sniffy'll round up some guys, he always does in a pinch."

And your brother said he's not going to be around," the old man said.

"How come you let him take off whenever he wants, huh dad?" I asked.

"That not true," he said.

"It practically is," I said.

"Ted's spending time on research over at Princeton. He says they work late over there, so it's easier for him if he stays overnight. And that way his buddies don't have to drive him home late at night. That'll all end when the school yeahr starts," the old man said.

"So can you call Sniffy?" I asked.

"I'll see what I can do," he said.

"Thanks, dad. I'd appreciate it."

As it turned out, Sniffy came through. The guys he hung out with usually needed the extra dough, so they were happy to fill in. I knew that after the lanes closed, they headed straight for the tavern to drink it all away. Sniffy's guys were ancient like him, but they worked steady and got the job done. I thought about the dream I'd had with all the dames smoking and drinking at the bar. Sniffy and his gang would go nuts over chicks like that.

The floor sweeper still gave me the chills. I guess I knew she had to be my old lady. I was trying to figure out what it all meant. I guess I was supposed to worry about the worst things that could happen, with the old man I mean.

I biked over to Jerry's. We strapped the sleeping bags to our bike racks, along with some snacks.

"It'll be dark about seven-fifteen, so if we hustle, they'll be some daylight left, " I said.

We got to her apartment by six-twenty. Sure enough, the woods I thought I'd seen were across the street. We walked our bikes in, and set them down.

"You remember any of those cars, Jerry?" I asked

"Can't say I do," he said.

"Damn, I wish I'd paid more attention. She's got to have a car. All we can do is wait. See if she goes out, or someone picks her up," I said.

"Or if she comes back from somewhere," Jerry said.

"Yeah, that too," I said. " I wonder if her place is in the front or back?"

"It's in the front, for sure," Jerry said. "I remember we went upstairs and made two lefts. I think her place is that one, to the left of the front door, the first one, not the second."

"I just hope she didn't see us running away," I said.

"We panicked, didn't we Danny?" Jerry asked.

"Yeah, plus you had to take a shit real bad," I said. We both laughed.

"Yeah, I wonder what she thought that was all about? You don't think she called the cops, do you?" Jerry asked.

"Nah, she knows you guys were just a couple of brainless dopes. But if she saw me, the ballgame's over."

"Don't you think she would have called your old man about it if she had?"

"Yeah, I suppose so," I said. "I had a funny dream the other night. You know how my old lady would clean up when

we closed?"

"Yeah."

"Well, in this dream, the old man dropped me off at the lanes, and he said he had a date, and Mr. Conrad was running the place. Turns out the lanes were closed down, and now the joint was just a bar. The bar was filled with these dames all dolled up and smoking and drinking away. And there was a woman sweeping the floor. She wouldn't let me see her face, but I knew it was supposed to be my old lady. Then the old man came in with that Tracy broad, the one we met the other night. Then she switched places with a dame at the bar, and the old man took this new dame out. I talked to Tracy, and she told me the old man was just like I'd written he was on that list. But then she said she dumped him on account of him having us two kids."

"That's crazy," Jerry said. "What about your mom? Did you talk to her?"

"She said to go away before the old man came back. She knew he was coming to pick up another dame. And at the end of the dream, the old lady disappeared, if that's who it was."

"Yeah, I wouldn't worry about it. The mind does weird stuff like that to you."

"I just think I'm going to keep having more dreams like that, until I know what's going to happen after the lanes close down, and what happens with the old man. Maybe I'm crazy to try and do this Jeannie thing, but I've got to help the old man, and she's right for him, even if it's a long shot."

A couple people came and went, but no Jeannie. It was getting nearly dark. My Timex said seven-twenty. The crickets were coming out, and Jerry slapped at his leg.

"Damn mosquitoes," he said.

"Let's get the sleeping bags. We'll wrap ourselves in them," I said.

"Good idea."

We did, and Jerry complained of being hot.

A minute later he said, "Jerry, it's her!"

Jeannie was coming down the entrance steps. She wore pants and a shirt. Nothing fancy. We watched her walk down the line of cars, and then open the door of a blue Ford. She got in, cranked it up, and took off.

"Well, now we know what car she drives," I said.

"Doesn't look like she's going on any date to me," Jerry said. "I mean, if she has a boyfriend, you'd think he'd be picking her up."

"Yeah, but you never know," I said. "Course whether she is or not, doesn't make any difference unless he comes back here."

"Well, we'll just have to wait it out. We figured we'd stay here all night anyway," Jerry said.

We sat in our sleeping bags. It was dark. The front of the apartment building was lit up, but not too great. I had to stay up until she came back.

It didn't help any when Jerry yawned, "So Danny, how you gonna get Jeannie and your old man together, anyway?"

"Maybe I'll have to talk to Ted, after all. I'll tell him my idea about getting them together, and see if he'll invite her over for dinner."

"What if Ted doesn't like the idea of them two getting to know each other?"

"I don't know why he wouldn't," I said.

"Trouble is," Jerry said, "if he doesn't like the idea, and then you get them together anyway, he'll know it was your doing, and he'll be mad as hell at you."

"Yeah, but so what? In the end he'll be happy. He told me she's important to him. At the awards, he got real angry at me because I told her and the awards guy about the satellite project I did."

"You did?"

"Yeah, and boy did he take it out on me when we got home. He tried to beat the crap out of me. He kept hitting me on the back of the head, and trying to turn me over, but I wouldn't let him. Anyway, Miss Jeannie's important to him, so he should like my idea."

"Ted's gotten real important, hasn't he?" Jerry asked.

"What do you mean?" I asked.

"Well, he doesn't work at the lanes anymore. He's off
instead doing his science shit, ain't he?"

"I asked him what he won his award for, and Miss Jeannie said it was for work he did on some kind of physics. She said the stuff was way over her head. Ted sure acted funny when he saw she had showed up. He looked like he was brainless. I guess he just freezes up when she's near him."

"Man, it would be something to have a girl like that, wouldn't it?" Jerry asked.

"Yeah, it sure would," I said.

"I don't think she's the kind of dame who would ever get the hots for a guy who owns a bowling alley, no offense to your old man," Jerry said.

"So what kind of guy would she go for?"

"A science guy, maybe?"

"A science guy," I said. "You gotta be kidding me. Why would she go for a boring kind of guy like that?"

"The world's changing, you said so yourself," Jerry said. "Atomic bombs and rockets and satellites."

"So, what's that got to do with anything and a dame? People get married to people who do stuff that has nothing to do with what they do. A dame just has to like a guy a whole lot, that's all."

"Yeah, maybe," Jerry said.

My Timex said nine-thirty. "Maybe she met some guy somewhere."

"Hey, maybe she drove to meet some broad," Jerry said.

"Maybe," I said.

Just then, a car came into the parking lot and pulled into Jeannie's spot.

"That's Jeannie's car, ain't it?" Jerry asked.

"Hard to tell, the light's so shitty, but that's gotta be it."

Both front doors opened.

"Hey, that's a guy getting out!" Jerry said.

"Yeah, how 'bout that?" I said. "Damn, I wish the light was better."

The two of them started walking up the steps to the front entrance. Miss Jeannie wrapped her arm around the guy's waist, and they disappeared inside. I wanted to be that guy so badly, I could scream.

"She's got a boyfriend, all right," Jerry said "Wonder if he'll stay all night."

"If he does, we'll be able to get a good look at him in the morning."

"Wonder why they came here in her car? I don't get it." Jerry said.

"Must be the lout doesn't have a car. Somehow I've got to make life miserable for him. Somehow I've got to get them to split up. Let's get some shut eye so we can wake up early."

I tried not to think about Jeannie as I lay in my sleeping bag, but it was no good. The thought of a guy with her all night made me sweat from jealousy. But what would I think if someday she hitched up with the old man? That would be okay, I told myself. She would deserve him, and he would deserve her. Nobody else on the planet should be touching my Jeannie.

I woke, and the day was brighter than I'd wanted it to be. My Timex said nine-thirty. I sat up and looked across at the parking lot. Miss Jeannie's blue Ford was gone.

23

"Hi, Danny," she said.

"Hi, Miss Jeannie."

"How do you think I look?"

I hadn't noticed what she was wearing. I looked her over. "I think you look beautiful," I croaked. I didn't know what shocked me more, what she had on or how delicious her body was.

"I'd let you touch me, but I can't," she said.

"You'd like me to touch you?" I asked.

"Maybe even more than that," she said.

"Really?"

"Really."

The scent of her perfume made my dizzy with desire.

"Well how come I can't?"

"I've got a boyfriend."

"I think I knew that. I saw you with him."

"He's nice, isn't he?" she asked. She fidgeted with her bra.

"I don't know, I just saw him from a distance."

"I'm waiting for him now."

"So what you're saying is, if it wasn't for this boyfriend, then I could be your boyfriend?" I asked.

"Maybe," she said. The smile she gave me made my blood boil.

"How did you meet this guy?" I asked.

"I don't remember. Does it matter?"

"I guess not," I said. *"Can you tell me where he lives?"*

"I could, but I won't."

"How come he doesn't have a car?"

"How did you know that?"

"'Cause we saw you come back here with him in your car."

"Mmmm, spying on me. How badly do you want me?" she asked.

"I don't know."

"I need a stronger commitment, if I'm going to take you seriously, Danny."

"I think I came here for my old man."

"What's he got to do with us, me?"

"I'm not sure," I said. *"It seems silly all of a sudden."*

"Do you want to know what appeals to me in a man?" she asked.

"Sure I do," I said. My knees went weak and I found a chair. She stood in front of me, her near nakedness driving me mad.

"I like someone like myself," she said.

"A science guy?"

She laughed and purred. *"Oh yes. That's why I was so impressed with your science project on satellites. How romantic."*

"So Jerry was right, then."

"Who is Jerry?" she asked.

"He was one of the guys who came to your door."

"Which one was he?"

The one who had to take a wicked crap," I told her.

"More spying," she said.

"I know. I just had to find out if you had a boyfriend."

"He'll be here soon, so you'll have to leave."

"What if he doesn't show up, what then?"

"I suppose you could stay. But he'll show."

"Wait a minute," I said. "How's he going to get here if he doesn't have a car?"

She looked confused. "I hadn't thought of that. How did you get here?"

"I rode my bike."

"How nice you would do that for me."

A knock came at the door. Miss Jeannie said, "I wonder who that could be?" She went to the door and looked through the peephole. "He's here!"

She opened the door. "How did you get here?" she asked the guy.

"I walked," the boyfriend said. He came into the apartment.

Who's this kid?" he asked.

"Oh, just a friend," Miss Jeannie said. "He'll be leaving."

I tried to focus on the boyfriend's face, but I couldn't.

"Jeannie can you leave us for a moment?" the boyfriend asked.

"Sure," she said and left.

"So what's your name?" he asked.

"Danny."

"Are you thinking of taking my place, is that it?" he asked.

"Why, if I say yes, will you let me?"

He laughed. "Of course not, you're just a kid."

"I know, that's what I said to myself, before I came here."

"Then why are you here?" he asked.

"I think I came for my old man, but now I'm not so sure. Miss Jeannie's so hot and all."

"You better believe it," the boyfriend said. He laughed and laughed. Dangling from his neck was a medal that said,

1957 Junior Achievement Award, Science

First Place

24

"I really appreciate this, Barry," I said. I leaned out the window, and caught the first hint of fall.

"Hey, no problem," he said. "So you got disqualified, huh? I guess me or Sam didn't put that earth sign on good enough."

"Ah, that's ok," I said. "Who gives a shit?"

We both laughed, and took a swig of our cream sodas.

"This stuff ain't too bad," said Barry. "So Ted kept telling you guys he was working all summer with us at Princeton huh?"

"Yeah, he sure did, son of a bitch. Turn up here." I said.

"Which way?" he asked.

"Left." I had Barry hang back far enough from the blue Ford, so Miss Jeannie wouldn't suspect a tail. I hadn't seen which way she'd turned, but I knew.

A few minutes later, we came to the gravel road. "Pull off here," I said.

I got out of the car, and walked the road until I saw the tree. Underneath it were two lovers, sitting on a cloth, having a picnic.

25

The news came that shocked the world. The Russkies had beaten us. Sputnik was up!

I made it to Yankee Stadium, that day of October fourth, can you believe it? I had finagled five World Series tickets on account of my lifetime pass. Don't ask me how I did it, for Christ's sake.

Jerry, Lance, the old man, Ted, and I were there, cheering on the Bronx Bombers for all we were worth.

I looked up at that October sky, and took a deep breath. I noticed the moon, hanging over the ballpark. I looked over at Ted. Yeah, while the rest of us science creeps had been all caught up in satellites, and now Sputnik, my brother had shot for the moon, and, son of a bitch, had made it.

THE END

The author welcomes comments and correspondence.

You can write him at
richardponcy@comcast.net